Simon Raven was born in London in 1927. He was educated at Charterhouse and King's College, Cambridge where he read Classics. After university, he joined the army as a regular officer in the King's Shropshire Light Infantry and saw service in Germany and Kenya where he commanded a Rifle Company. In 1957 he resigned his commission and took up book reviewing. His first novel, *The Feathers of Death*, was published in 1959. Since then he has written many reviews, general essays, plays for radio and television as well as the scripts for a number of successful television series including *Edward and Mrs Simpson* and *Love in a Cold Climate* plus a host of novels. The highly acclaimed ALMS FOR OBLIVION sequence is published by Grafton Books in chronological order. The sequence takes its title from a passage in Shakespeare's *Troilus and Cressida*, has been referred to as 'a latter-day Waugh report on another generation of Bright Young Things', and has been compared favourably with the *romans fleuves* of Anthony Powell and C. P. Snow. With the publication in 1984 of *Morning Star* he began a new novel series under the title THE FIRST-BORN OF EGYPT. It is a sequel to ALMS FOR OBLIVION. Simon Raven lives and works in Deal, Kent.

G000275467

By the same author

Novels

The Feathers of Death
Brother Cain
Doctors Wear Scarlet
The Roses of Picardie
Close of Play
An Inch of Fortune

The ALMS FOR OBLIVION sequence,
in chronological order:

Fielding Gray
Sound the Retreat
The Sabre Squadron
The Rich Pay Late
Friends in Low Places
The Judas Boy
Places Where They Sing
Come Like Shadows
Bring Forth the Body
The Survivors

THE FIRST-BORN OF EGYPT

Morning Star
The Face of the Waters
Before the Cock Crow

Belles-Lettres

The English Gentleman
Boys Will Be Boys
The Fortunes of Fingel

Plays

Royal Foundation and Other Plays

Autobiography

Shadows on the Grass

SIMON RAVEN

New Seed for Old

The First-born of Egypt: Volume 4

GRAFTON BOOKS
A Division of the Collins Publishing Group

LONDON GLASGOW
TORONTO SYDNEY AUCKLAND

Grafton Books
A Division of the Collins Publishing Group
8 Grafton Street, London W1X 3LA

Published by Grafton Books 1989

First published in Great Britain by
Frederick Muller 1988

ISBN 0-586-20019-3

Printed and bound in Great Britain by
Collins, Glasgow

Set in Times

Queen of this Universe, doe not believe
Those rigid threats of Death; ye shall not Die:
How should ye? By the Fruit? It gives you Life
To Knowledge: By the Threat'ner? look on mee,
Mee who have touch'd and tasted, yet doth live,
And life more perfect have attaind than Fate
Meant mee, by venturing higher than my Lot.

Milton, *Paradise Lost*: Book IX 684–690
(The Serpent to the Woman)

PART ONE
The Singles Match

'Of course,' said the Marchioness Canteloupe, 'Eton Fives is a game for four. One pair against another.'

'I know, my lady,' said Marius Stern.

'You call me "Thea". We have, when all is said, known each other for some time. We were both at Sarum's Christening, for a start.'

'How is Sarum?'

'You will soon see for yourself. His nurse, Daisy, will bring him in his pram to the Fives Court during our game.'

The Fives Court in the Marquess Canteloupe's Wiltshire house was at one end of the Great Court, which they must traverse to reach it. Theodosia Canteloupe's long and generous legs, dressed in trousers of real flannel gone slightly yellow, carried her so easily and swiftly over the marble paving that Marius, though his legs too were long and fluent, had quite a job to keep up. He started to sweat, just a little, in the April sun. When they reached the Fives Court, Thea said,

'I'm going to play in shorts.'

She took off her trousers, to show a very brief pair of running shorts. Marius goggled at her huge, smooth thighs.

'If you're going to examine my legs so thoroughly,' said Thea, 'you might at least let me see yours.'

Marius had dressed himself for their game in a cricket shirt and grey slacks.

'I'm sorry,' he now said earnestly, 'but I've no pants on

9

under my greys. You see, at School, when we're playing games, we're not allowed to wear underpants under our shorts or trousers.'

'I shan't mind that. You've got your shirt.'

Marius giggled. 'I'm afraid it's rather short,' he said.

'Is it? I always thought those cricket shirts had enormous flaps, back *and* front. We found a trunk full of my father's, after he died. They were absolutely voluminous.'

'They aren't made like that any more. The manufacturers are far too mingy.'

'I still shan't mind,' she said.

'But . . . Sarum . . . and his nurse?'

'You can put your trousers on when we see them coming across the Great Court.'

'But now there's someone else coming . . .'

And so there was. Leonard Percival, Lord Canteloupe's Private Secretary, though his ulcer was playing him up something rotten and he felt about a thousand years old, had nevertheless decided to come out into the fresh air and the sun; and now, seeing that something was in train in the Eton Fives Court, he was wandering along for a gander.

'In that case,' said Theodosia with quiet loathing, 'I'll let you off until later.'

'I'm afraid . . . mine . . . are a bit thin.'

'You're only fifteen and odd months. They'll fill out.'

She started to put on her flannels.

'Mr Percival,' she said, 'is inclined to lech. Since singles aren't really pukka at this game, shall we just knock up? Or would you like to play for points?'

'Let's play for points, my 1 – er, Thea. I know they don't recognize singles at Eton Fives but I used to have super games with . . . with someone at School.'

'With your friend, Palairet,' said Thea.

Marius sat down on the step that divided the lower from the upper court.

'Oh, Christ,' he said. 'Why wasn't I kinder to him . . . when he was here, Thea? I'd hardly spoken to him in months when he was killed.'

'His aunt told me it was a blessing. There was no money left. Certainly not enough to keep him at School. One parent had died very suddenly. The other was rotten with cancer. The aunt would have done what she could for him, but that would have been precious little. She'd lost most of her money in some swindle on Lloyd's.'

'Still, to die like that at fifteen – '

' – He died very gallantly.'

'That's all very well,' said Marius. '"Here lie we because we did not choose/ To shame the mother-land from which we sprung./ Life, to be sure, is nothing much to lose,/ But young men think it is, and we were young."'

'He's dead,' said Theodosia flatly. 'Like all of us, he's better dead. Now forget it. Let's get going before we have to talk to Mr Percival. I'll throw the ball up.' She lumbered lightly on to the upper step. 'Love all.'

Pity she's not wearing those shorts, thought Leonard Percival, as he approached and glinted into the Fives Court. That Stern boy should strip well too. You stupid old cunt, you. You couldn't get a rise if they started fucking on the floor right in front of you. For some minutes he imagined this, and did not get a rise.

'Five all,' called Marius.

He threw the ball up for Theodosia to cut it, caught the swing on the volley with both hands cupped, and patted the ball into the left-hand angle of the upper court. Theodosia, now up there with him, rather sweaty beside him, scooped the ball hard against the front wall so that it sailed back, high but drooping, then seemed to stop dead in the air and plummet vertically, landing just behind the buttress and spinning straight into it, thus making it impossible for Marius, though he was now down on the lower court, to return it.

'You should have got it left-handed as it came down,' said Theodosia, 'before it fell behind the box. Good practice for your left hand.'

'I wasn't quite there in time.'

'Get those thin legs moving quicker.'

Thin legs, thought Leonard Percival: how does she know?

'Still five all, Thea. You to go up.'

Thea mounted the step to the upper court. Marius turned and walked well down the lower court, so that he might get a good running swinge at the ball. A red-haired girl, whom he just remembered from the day of Sarum's Christening, was wheeling a black pram towards him. The pram's hood was up, reminding Marius of a photograph that he had seen of a London cab, taken just after the war.

'Go and say hallo to Sarum,' Theodosia called.

Sarum. Sarum of Old Sarum. Canteloupe's heir by his dead wife, Baby, Marius thought. Theodosia's stepson. He remembered the fine, lusty, bellowing and beshitten infant whom Sarum's grandfather, Sir Thomas Llewyllyn, had fully immersed in the Font of Lancaster College Chapel.

'In the Name of the Father, and of the Son, and of the Holy Ghost,' Sir Thomas had boomed (washing away the excreta with Sarum's Christening shawl), 'I here baptize thee: Tullius Fielding d'Azincourt' – at this stage he had raised the newly cleansed baby high in the air above him – 'Llewyllyn Gregory Jean-Josephine Maximin Sarum

Detterling, henceforth to be called, by courtesy of England, Lord Sarum of Old Sarum. AMEN.'

Three years ago that had been. Sarum of Old Sarum. Little Tully Sarum.

'Hullo, Tully,' he said, putting his face round the hood of the pram.

An ancient gnome's face drooled back at him.

Of course, thought Marius. A three-year-old boy, on a lovely day like this: he should be walking, hand in hand with his nanny.

He looked at the pretty ginger nurse.

'I like to think,' she said, 'that the real Tully was taken by the little folk, and this was what they left in exchange.'

There was a nasty little hiss from inside the hood.

'Now he knows,' Theodosia thought.

'Why did she show him?' Leonard Percival thought.

This boy at least has grown well since the Christening, the ginger nanny thought.

'Come on, Marius,' called Theodosia. 'Five all. Me to throw up.'

Captain the Marquess Canteloupe and his friend, Major Giles Glastonbury, sat on the balcony of the Pavilion at Lord's, savouring the first match of the season. Normally, at this time of the year, it would have been cold, damp and probably windy for ill measure; but this afternoon was warm and grateful, a day of all days to sit talking in the open with a friend.

'Tully's a stumer,' Canteloupe said; 'something's gone badly wrong.'

13

'I remember,' said Glastonbury, his black eyebrows flaring, 'that his behaviour last Christmas was rather odd.'

'Things have got a lot worse since then. The worse they get, the faster they get still worse. Someone ought to teach this boy to hold his bat properly. Look at his left hand – screwed round the handle like a clamp. He'll never hit the ball clean if he lives to be a hundred.'

'They like to do things their own way these days,' Glastonbury said, 'even if it's the wrong one. They don't take lessons any more.'

'Which is why most of 'em are so bloody awful, I suppose. Overpaid and pampered, and won't listen when they're told. He can't talk, Tully can't. He can't or won't walk – that nurse of his has to carry him everywhere. He's beginning to look quite horrible – like a mummy. Bad blood on his mother's side, of course.'

'What are you going to do?'

'Get another.'

Glastonbury let this pass in silence. He knew, and knew that Canteloupe knew he knew, that Canteloupe could never now 'get' an heir in the biblical sense. Whether, where and how he might *procure* one was another matter.

'It's a question,' Canteloupe said, 'of getting Theodosia pregnant. There could be an answer. That's why I'm in London.'

He spoke as if he had come up to see some specialist who would instruct him in the process of fertilizing his wife. In fact, however, as Giles Glastonbury well knew, he was giving Glastonbury an oblique and confidential hint: he was admitting that he was going to cheat, that he had come up to London to leave Theodosia free to take the necessary steps with the least possible embarrassment. Anyhow, who the hell cares, thought Glastonbury. From all I hear, from all he himself has implied from time to

14

time, he seems to have cheated over Sarum. Let him do the same again. What does it matter who's the next Marquess Canteloupe? That party's over now, much as we may wish it wasn't.

'And the best of luck,' he said aloud. 'But even if you get Theodosia to drop another, you'll still have Sarum on your hands.'

'Yes,' said Canteloupe. 'I want to consult you about that. About the possibilities.'

He broke off to applaud a pretty catch which dismissed the young man with the ugly grip. Though he was clearly out (caught by second slip), the young man did not budge. He stood until the bowler appealed; and then, when the umpire raised his finger, he pretended not to notice. Finally, when the captain of the fielding side had directed his attention to the umpire, who now raised his finger a second time, the young batsman bristled with affront, as though all his human rights had suddenly been denied him, slammed his bat against his pad, and slouched off the field, scowling and blinking.

'Tell me,' said Canteloupe, 'have you heard anything of Fielding Gray?'

Glastonbury, who had been expecting Canteloupe to dilate on the 'possibilities' to which he had just referred, wondered what train of thought had prompted the question. The disposal of Sarum could hardly be a matter for Fielding Gray. Or could it?

'Why do you ask, Canteloupe?'

'That young fellow's filthy behaviour reminded me of Fielding. He once carried on just like that during an Army Match at Camberley. Regimental cricket week – game against the Ramblers. Happened just before I sent my papers in. True, Fielding had made 99 and almost certainly wasn't out – he was given l.b.w. by some cunt of a

15

desk General, who insisted on getting into the act and umpiring – to an off-break that pitched outside the leg stump. Still, it was thought that Fielding should not have displayed such nasty temper.'

'No more he should. He was always rather hairy at the heel. Not his fault, of course. His father was a small businessman in Wisbech and his mother's people were bakers. As for what he's doing just now, last I heard was that he'd left for a tour of the Far East with young Jeremy Morrison – you know, Peter Morrison's son.'

'Luffham, he's called now – '

' – Oh yes? – '

' – Luffham of Whereham. I thought young Jeremy had pretty well dropped Fielding.'

'Come to think of it, Fielding seemed to be saying something of the sort when we came to you last Christmas. But I suppose they could have made it up. I saw them together at a race meeting a little while back. Bellhampton.'

And I saw a lot else there too, thought Giles. But we won't open up *that* box of blowflies just now. As for these 'possibilities' Canteloupe wants to consult me about, it looks as if he's forgotten . . . for the time being at least. Bloody good job too – if he means what I think he means. But of course if anyone *can* manage a thing of that sort, it's Canteloupe and I. A bit like the old days in India – though I must say, that poor little brute of a Tully Sarum would make a pretty pathetic target.

* * *

'You win fifteen-twelve,' conceded Marius to Theodosia, 'and take the match by three games to two.' He remembered the audience that had assembled earlier, and shuddered. But when he came out of the Fives Court he saw that nurse and pram were gone, and that Leonard Percival was crawling away towards the far end of the Great Court.

'Come on,' said Theodosia; 'time for a bath.'

She looked at Percival, in his slow retreat, then lowered her voice, for the ex-secret agent (or 'Jermyn Street man', as he preferred to be called) had, she knew, a very sharp sense of hearing, however decrepit the rest of him.

'I want you to come and have your bath with me,' she said.

Marius allowed this intelligence to sink in.

'So that you can look at my legs?' he said.

'You may think I'm being very peculiar this afternoon – '

' – Very exciting, Thea – '

' – Perhaps not so exciting after all. But certainly peculiar. I shall explain.'

They crossed the Great Court in silence and went up a back staircase, into a small dressing room littered with white sweaters, Royal Tennis racquets and photographs of small white-flannelled groups.

'This was Baby Canteloupe's boudoir,' said Theodosia. 'There were some pretty things in it, but when I came here I turfed them out. Women always do that, you know: they always change the way things were left by their predecessors. Most men don't care or even notice. What did you make of Sarum?'

'I . . . I thought he was too old for that pram.'

'A very delicate way of putting it.'

17

She unfastened the top of his slacks and pulled them down over his knees.

'Yes,' she said; 'too thin to be perfect, but only just. This too – though I can't speak as an expert. How did you get that little scar?'

'When I was circumcised.'

'Look,' she said, 'I'm hating this.' Her cheek reddened along the broad, high cheekbone. 'And I don't understand anything about it. But I thought, we'll have a bath together, and see each other, and then it will happen. He'll like it like that, I thought.'

'And so I should.'

'But I can't go through with it, Marius. The only reason I'm doing this is to give Canteloupe an heir. You saw Sarum – there has to be another heir. What I want you to do is to . . . put your seed into me, as quickly as possible, and there an end of it.'

'Thea. There has to be kindness first. I can't just stick this into you and come. It would be horrible. Anyhow, I *can't* do it like that. Nor could you. Jenny explained it all to me. You have to *want* me to come in.'

'Who's Jenny?'

'A stable lass. Head stable lass. Where I worked earlier these hols. She showed me. She was kind to me and showed me how to be kind to her . . . how to be kind to you,
Thea.'

'You don't understand. I don't . . . want . . . any of this kindness. It would . . . drag me down, soil and weaken me. I want my badminton and my tennis. *Clean* things. That's what I want to do with my limbs and my body. Not this.'

'But you say you have to do this,' said Marius, 'to give your husband a new son?'

18

'Yes. I promised him.'

'Then this once at least you have to do this with me. Can't we make it nice, Thea? Something we shall like to remember? Just this once?'

'I can't . . . make it nice. I was going to try. But I can't.'

'Then let me try. Go into the bathroom, Thea. Run the bath and get into it. Then call me.'

'And you'll try,' she said bleakly, 'you'll try the tricks this Jenny taught you.'

'I shall try to make you feel how beautiful I find you.'

The huge bath had ample room for both. Thea lay, rigid at first, while Marius floated beside her and washed her. Funny, she thought: no one ever washed me kindly before. My adoptive mother hated us, and all those girls she hired had unkind hands. She must have known they would have and picked them on purpose, because there were so many of them (since none would stay long in the same house as my mother) that sooner or later there must have been one that had kind hands unless she was deliberately choosing only those that hadn't. She would have been very good at that: she would have known instinctively. But now . . . this little boy . . . is washing me as tenderly as my mother should have done.

She closed her eyes and eased her limbs in the bath.

'Galahad,' she murmured; 'Galahad.'

For a moment Marius ceased soaping her thighs. Galahad, he thought: wasn't Palairet called Galahad? He never let anyone use the name, we all called him 'Pally', but once he told me. 'What does your "G" stand for?' I asked him. 'I'll tell *you* if you promise not to tell anyone else,' he said. So, thought Marius, as he began to soap Theodosia's slightly parted thighs again, on the inside now, waiting for them to part still further, not hurrying,

19

not insisting, just letting the intimation of sweet desire flow gently through his fingers as gap-toothed Jenny had taught him – so, thought Marius, Thea thinks, or is imagining, that I am poor dead Pally. She must have liked him . . . and chosen me for this because I was once close to him. Well, let her think, or imagine, what pleases her best.

'Thea, Thea,' he whispered in her ear; 'lovely Thea.'

'Galadad . . . Yes, Galahad . . . Yes, Galahad . . . Oh, yes.'

After the day's cricket was over, Canteloupe took Glastonbury to dine in his club, the last one in London which would in no circumstances admit a woman, not even in a menial capacity.

'Not a bad afternoon's play as things go nowadays,' Canteloupe said. 'Pity that young MCC batsman had to behave so foully when he was caught. Replacement needed there, I think.'

He brooded for a minute or two, until the lobster mousse arrived.

'Replacements,' he said. 'If one chap don't suit, you get another. Tully don't suit, so I'm going to get another.'

'So you said this afternoon.'

'But then, as *you* said this afternoon, one still has a problem. The replacement may be as sound as you could wish, but you've still got the original. You've still got Tully. The first-born. The official heir.'

'Precisely.'

'So what do you do about that?'

20

'You send him to a discreet nursing home,' said Glastonbury, 'where he contracts pneumonia, as imbecile infants are prone to.'

'That's what I thought,' said Canteloupe. 'So I got in touch with La Soeur. He's been making . . . discreet medical arrangements . . . for all of us ever since I can remember. Could he, I asked, take Tully into permanent care? And La Soeur put on a po-face and said: "In the old days, as I think you know, Tullius would almost certainly have died of pneumonia. As things are now, you need not worry. Such children are very carefully immunized and attended." "Oh, are they?" I said. "So I go on paying a thousand guineas a week until he dies of old age?" "There are nosey-parkers," said La Soeur, obviously sick of the goody-goody act and seeing no need to prolong it with an old chum like me, "there are snoopers and pokers and pryers and delators, who are determined that every life, no matter how painful, hopeless or degraded, shall be preserved as long as possible – often far beyond its natural termination. What their motive is, no one quite knows. It *cannot* be humanitarian . . . to sustain lives that can yield only agony and humiliation. Perhaps, in the case of patients who were once rich or beautiful or both, the motive is to punish them for the privilege they have enjoyed. But however that may be," said La Soeur, "spies and meddlers there are everywhere who make damaging – ruinous – official complaints if any patient dies a day before he absolutely has to. In the case of Tullius, there are now drugs which will positively keep him alive, *despite* the factors – decay or atrophy, due to inaction, of certain systems, functions and organs – which would formerly have killed him of pneumonia or some related disorder. If, by some unhappy chance, I should

21

neglect to see that these drugs were regularly administered, then informers might well inform on me and even I, with all my experience, could not survive the consequence."

'"But surely," I said, "you don't allow these informers, these snoopers and the rest, into *your* Nursing Home?"

'"I can't keep them out," La Soeur said. "One never knows who they are – until they act. The most modest, sensible and obedient of probationary nurses, engaged by the most clear-eyed of Matrons, may suddenly turn out to be a fanatical preserver of worthless life."'

Canteloupe's fastidious mouth drooped deeply with frustration and distaste.

'Well,' said Glastonbury, 'that puts the kybosh on that.'

Both men ate silently through gulls' eggs and stuffed quails, and drank efficiently through white Châteauneuf-du-Pape and red Montrachet, until at length Glastonbury remarked:

'All this talk of La Soeur reminds me of something.'

'Talk of La Soeur reminds everyone of something . . . generally an expensive late abortion or a nasty clap.'

'One of La Soeur's minor rackets,' said Glastonbury, 'was getting chaps out of National Service. For a straight hundred (good money in those days) he'd fit you up with flat feet or chronic incontinence or *something* that all the other doctors had somehow overlooked. But in one case, so I once heard, he refused to do this. Fellow in question was Raisley Conyngham . . .'

' – Racehorse owner? Beak at my old School? – '

' – That's the chap.'

'Why did La Soeur turn down Conyngham?'

'In the end, you know, La Soeur is a thoroughly *decent* sort of man. He tries to bring about those things which will, as he sees it, improve the quality of life all round.

His speciality, you might say, is – or certainly was – the disposal of incommoding and unsightly human litter. Now, the story runs that La Soeur took against Raisley – some kind of instinct.'

'Didn't like the cut of his jib?'

'It went deeper than that. La Soeur scented some sort of evil, or moral poison, in the very centre of Raisley's being. So he wouldn't get Raisley out of his National Service, though Raisley offered ten times the usual fee. "The best thing that can happen to you," La Soeur said to Raisley, "is a timely accident with a grenade or whatever that blows your cunting head off. Or perhaps your fellow recruits will take one sniff and rend you to pieces. All ways round, National Service is about the best chance of getting rid of you, Conyngham, a slim chance but the best I know of. Come to that, it might even be worth a small war."'

'But in fact,' said Canteloupe, 'Conyngham surely did quite well in the Army? Didn't he get a National Service Commission?'

'Yes,' said Glastonbury, 'but only because I put in a word for him. They were going to fail him – lack of guts on some manoeuvre – but I managed all that for him at the War House.'

'Why did you trouble?'

'My cousin Prideau asked me. He'd been thick with Raisley at Cambridge. And I thought at the time: Now you'll *owe* me, Raisley boy. One day *I'll* have something that needs fixing, something in *your* area as this biz is in mine, and then I'll come asking.'

'That was some time ago. *Have* you . . . gone asking?'

'Oh, yes. And been very handsomely answered. At my request, Raisley engaged that poor old Sozzler Jack Lamprey to train his horses. As it happened, I was doing him a good turn: Jack has been a success there. So now he may be inclined to do me another favour or two. After all,' said Glastonbury (who came within spitting distance of calling cousins with the Queen), 'I might very well be in a position to repay him.'

'And you think . . . ?' said Canteloupe hopefully.

'. . . I think that if any man in the kingdom can arrange the necessary and painless extinction, without fuss, suspicion or even notice, of Tullius, Baron Sarum of Old Sarum, that man is called Raisley Conyngham.'

'The highly respected schoolmaster? How would *he* go about such dirty work?'

'I said "*arrange*", Canteloupe. Conyngham is no Tyrrel. But from what I know of the man, and what cousin Prideau has told me, he will understand your predicament; he will wish to oblige us both; he will appreciate the aesthetic and social improprieties of one such as Tullius inheriting a fine Marquisate; and he will recommend or set in motion an immaculate series of entirely humdrum events . . . which will end in the desired yet almost unperceived result.'

At Waterloo Station, Marius rang up the Stern house in Chelsea, having not had time to do this before leaving Wiltshire. To his great relief the only present inhabitant, the cook, answered the telephone.

'Stern residence,' said the cook.

Is it Ethel he likes to be called, Marius now wondered, or Mavis? It was so long since he had been there that he had clean forgotten.

'Marius here, Ethel,' he said at a venture.

'Oh, Master Marius, is it really you? I thought no one was ever coming here again. By the way, I've changed my name to Crystal. More refined.'

'Well, Crystal,' said Marius, 'it is really me, and I'd like to spend a couple of nights. I've had to leave somewhere unexpectedly early.'

'No trouble, sir, I hope?'

'No. Just a . . . misunderstanding. I know it's a bit late, but can you fix me up with some dinner?'

'It will be a *pleasure*, Master Marius. I've been turning into a dreadful slut with no one to cook for. How about . . . Oeufs Mornay and Entrecôte Marchand de Vin?'

Better than I'd have got down at Canteloupe's house, thought Marius. The kitchen there was getting very slovenly ('sluttish', as Crystal might say) to judge from the luncheon he'd had on his arrival there earlier in the day. From that point of view, he thought as he climbed into a taxi, he was glad to be out of the place.

'You must go now,' Thea had said as they lay in the tepid bath.

'All right. What time's dinner?'

'I meant, go altogether. Leave the house. Now. I'll give you money.'

'I have my own, my lady.'

'And somewhere to go?'

'Of course,' he said, thinking that he would return to Raisley Conyngham and Milo Hedley at Ullacote.

'Go there. Otherwise this might happen again. It must not happen again. I feel dirty and altogether diminished.'

'But surely,' Marius had said, 'if you're to have a good chance of . . . getting what you and Canteloupe want . . . it ought to happen again. Several times.'

'I must hope that once has been enough. If not, then I

25

shall have to think what to do. I promise you, Marius,' she said, touching his wrist quite kindly, 'that if it has to happen again it shall be nobody but you. But as it is, unless I find it absolutely necessary, I never wish to sink into that horrible condition . . . of non-mind, non-will, non-control . . . ever again.'

'But Thea, you did keep control, more's the pity. You were going to come . . . I know you were going to come, just after I did, I *felt* it . . . but you stopped yourself, you thrust me away.'

'Yes. Because you made that noise. You sort of – sort of squealed. Horrible. That brought me to my senses, gave me my sanity back before I suffered the same humiliation. But even so there had already been much too much of my own whimpering and whining. You are very beguiling, Marius. Is that the work of the woman, Jenny?'

'She showed me. I wanted to show you. Why did you call me "Galahad"?'

'Did I? You see what I mean about non-mind? If I could confuse you with Galahad Palairet . . .'

'You loved him, didn't you?'

'Yes. And I'm very fond of you. But go now. *Go*. Mr Percival will arrange a taxi to the station.'

As indeed Mr Percival had, civilly and without comment. He had also construed the timetable. There were no convenient trains to Minehead or Taunton, he had said; Marius would have to change three times and arrive well after 2 A.M. It was then that Marius had decided to go to London instead of Ullacote. This would probably not please Raisley and Milo, who were expecting him to go straight from Canteloupe's house, after spending the two nights for which he had been invited, to School, where the Cricket Quarter was to begin the day after the next. But clearly, since that arrangement was now out, some other must be come to. Marius strongly supposed that Raisley would have expected him, in these new circumstances, either to return to Ullacote, as he had at first intended, or at least to consult him on the telephone. But he was no longer a child, thought Marius, and he would now show himself and anyone else who might be interested that he was perfectly capable, at a need, of making his own decisions. If he went to London for two nights, he would have a good opportunity to visit the family lawyer, 'Young' John Groves, whom he wished to consult about money, of which his mother, in her new roles of socialist and miser, was trying to keep him short – so far without success, but she was a persistent woman, and he must make sure that 'Young' John Groves wasn't going to be got at. He also had another scheme, a scheme connected with what had passed down at Canteloupe's but not as yet fully thought out.

When Marius arrived at the house in Chelsea, Crystal said:

'My word, we are looking bonny. Dinner in half an hour, when you've had a nice bath.'

'Thank you, Crystal. You're very kind.'

'Not at all. It's such a joy to see one of the family again. Miss Rosie always stays at that hotel when she's in London, and your lady mother hasn't been here . . . since I don't know when. Talking of whom, Master Marius, I must have a quiet word in your ear – when you've had your dinner, of course.'

The telephone rang. Crystal answered it.

'It's a Mr Milo Hedley, sir, for you.'

'How did you know I was here?' Marius said.

'We shall aways know, Marius,' Milo Hedley said. 'In this case Raisley happened to telephone Lady Canteloupe to make sure you'd settled in all right, and she said you'd had to go. So I guessed where. Why did you have to go?'

'Lady Canteloupe was worried and unhappy about something.'

'I see. She doesn't like her work. Did you do yours?'

'I tried my best.'

'Good. Then here's Raisley for you.'

'. . . Ah, Marius,' said Raisley Conyngham in his sweet and plummy voice. 'So how shall you fill the time before returning to School?'

'I must see my lawyer in London, sir. Then I was thinking of a trip down to Cambridge tomorrow.' I might as well own up straightaway, Marius thought. Mr Conyngham will find out anyway.

'With anything particular in mind?'

'I'd like to see Lancaster College again.'

This was only part of the truth, but it would serve.

'Excellent. You go with my blessing. And Marius: you might do yourself a good turn by calling on Sir Tom Llewyllyn. After all, he is your uncle by marriage, one might say, and your father was one of his oldest friends. I hear Sir Tom has not been very well lately, so telephone his Lodging before you go there.'

Without further remark, or even a form of farewell, Raisley Conyngham rang off. Now I'll *have* to go and see Sir Thomas, Marius thought. But perhaps he'll be too ill to see anybody. And in any case, there's really plenty of time both for that *and* the other thing.

* * *

'How shall I approach Conyngham?' said Canteloupe, as he and Glastonbury sat down at one of the Backgammon tables.

'When, in the normal course of events, would you next go down to your School at Farncombe?' Glastonbury said.

'To see the first decent cricket match which the XI is playing at home.'

'Right. Take me with you when you go. I'll introduce you to Raisley Conyngham – and help with the conversation if needed. He'll be very quick to take our meaning, as I told you at dinner. What do we play for these days?' he said, setting up the pieces.

'A hundred a point.'

'Make it two,' said Glastonbury, who was conscious of having rendered and promised important services for which, as he invariably beat Canteloupe, he would now be very well paid.

'The thing is, Master Marius,' said Crystal as he served Marius with coffee, 'that my wages ain't being paid any more. Nor haven't been for several months.'

'Who should pay them? The lawyer?'

'No. Your mother. Every month she sends me a cheque from France. Or rather, she used to. There's been nothing since Christmas.'

'No notice of dismissal?'

'No, sir. Just nothing.'

'My mother,' said Marius with a pleasurable sense of disloyalty, 'is going through a nasty patch of meanness. She's obviously forgetting your wages on purpose. In which case it will become harder and harder to get the arrears out of her. I have to see Mr Groves, the solicitor, tomorrow. I'll try and arrange it all with him, so that there'll be no more mistakes for the future. And now, Crystal, is there such a thing as a glass of port about the place?'

Theodosia Canteloupe walked across the Great Court in the moonlight and stood for a while in the Fives Court.

It was like being possessed, she thought. Mindless, like an animal; thank God I managed to hold back at the end. Please God his seed has already taken and there need be no more coupling. And yet, she thought, he was so beautiful. If Palairet was Galahad, Marius is Achilles. Achilles . . . to be admired, adored even, but not fondled and paddled on, nor rubbed against and frotted on, until both of us become beasts, and the two beasts become one, the beast with two backs. Never for me Achilles the panting fornicator, but Achilles the warrior. Achilles, son of Peleus, she thought; 'Achilles his Armour'. Where did that come from? From Sir Thomas Browne, she thought. And then she remembered the old story (which Canteloupe and she had read together in the *Iliad* during the early days of their marriage) about the forging of that armour, how Thetis came to Hephaestus to ask it as a boon, and how Hephaestus wrought the shield: '"Therein he wrought the earth,"' she quoted softly to herself, leaning against the buttress of the Fives Court, '"therein the heavens"' – she stepped out of the Fives Court and looked up at the sky (just as she had done that time with

Canteloupe, as they sat reading together on the balcony in Navplion), picking out, as she spoke the names, such of the stars as she could find above her – '"the Pleiades, and the Hyades (the Raining Ones) and the mighty hunter, Orion, and the Bear, that men also call the Wain, that circleth ever in its own place, and watcheth Orion the hunter, and alone has no part in the baths of Ocean."'

'Who,' said Marius to 'Young' John Groves in his chambers in Lincoln's Inn, 'were my father's executors?'

Outside, the sun was shining on grass and river: in John Groves's chambers there was a dank gloom as if Cocytus were flowing through the room.

'Your father's executors,' said 'Young' John Groves in a voice like the sound of a vice tightening on metal, 'were your mother, Lord Canteloupe and myself.'

'What's Canteloupe got to do with it?'

'He was your father's partner in the publishing firm.'

'Well, look, sir,' said Marius. 'My mother is being stupid and difficult. Let us charitably call it the change of life. She has become unbelievably mean with money, and excuses herself by talking socialism. We must behave just like anyone else, she says, even if it does make us miserable, in order not to take advantage or cause offence.'

'That kind of thing is very much in the air,' 'Young' John Groves ground out.

'So, first: she can't, I hope, reduce or cancel my allowance?'

'No. The annual amount you are to receive, increasing

as you grow older and periodically adjustable in the same ratio as inflation, is laid down in your father's will and *must* be paid to you until you are twenty-one – at which time, of course, you will inherit a capital sum.'

'And no malicious person can prevent this – not even an executor acting "in my own interest"?'

'Your mother has already tried,' grated 'Young' John Groves, 'on the grounds that so large an allowance to so young a person was "socially and morally unacceptable".'

'I don't know that it's as large as all that,' said Marius. 'What did you tell her?'

'That I am not a moralist but a lawyer.'

'So that's all right. Now, second: my mother has ceased to pay the cook at the London house. What's to do about that, sir?'

'Nothing that I know of.'

'It's important that the place should be kept going.'

'I thought none of you went there?'

'Very seldom. It is, nevertheless, a convenient *pied-à-terre*. And Crystal, the cook, has deserved well of the family.'

'There is a fund available to you, on which you may draw, with my approval, for emergencies and unexpected contingencies. If your mother is so – ah – variable, you could pay *her* (Crystal the cook, I mean) out of this fund yourself, thus stabilizing the situation.'

'Him.'

'Who?'

'Crystal the cook.'

'Crystal is his surname, I apprehend.'

'No. He just likes to be called Crystal. Sometimes he wears a skirt. He cooks even better when he wears a skirt, though he also cooks deliciously in trousers. Will you please write to him, sir, pay him the arrears he's owed since 1 January, and tell him that from now on he'll be paid by you. Don't mention me.'

'I must know (a) his surname and (b) the amount he has been receiving.'

'I know neither. Ring up the house, please, and ask him.'

'Very well, Marius. You'll have to sign an authority. I shall give my approval, as you obviously feel strongly about this; but I warn you: if you are to continue paying – ah – Crystal's wages, it will use up most of the interest annually generated by your emergency fund.'

(And I shall lose the interest on the interest, he thought: but this boy must be humoured; he stands to be an important client later.)

'A pity and a nuisance, but it can't be helped,' said Marius. 'Last of all, sir: please write to my mother and tell her she need no longer pay the cook, as other arrangements have been made. And I hope that makes her ashamed of herself. Only nothing can. Nothing ever could,' he said, rather gleefully.

'Your mother's father, Sir Edwin Turbot, now mercifully deceased,' said 'Young' John Groves, 'was reputed the most shameless man in the Lower House, with the exception of Winston Churchill.'

'My mother sometimes speaks of him even now,' said Marius. 'It seems he used to cram whole crumpets or muffins into his mouth, and then swallow them unchewed, like a boa constrictor.'

'Young' John Groves laughed, as merry, thought Marius, as a leper's bell. Anticipating Groves's rising to give him his *congé*, he himself rose first to mark his status. This gruesome old man was his paid servant: it was for him, Marius, to indicate when the discussion was at an end.

It was now just before noon, he read from 'Young' John Groves's sepulchral clock: he could have his luncheon on the train and be in Cambridge by half past two . . . in good time for everything.

Carmilla Salinger, Lady Canteloupe's twin sister, was a junior history don in Lancaster and had a set of rooms in Sitwell's Building, from one window of which she could look down, to her left, albeit at a very sharp angle (north by east), at the South Door of the Chapel. This is what Carmilla was doing, standing tall and easy at the window, when Marius knocked on her door at a quarter to three.

'Marius Stern,' she said, as he came in.

'Miss Salinger.'

"Carmilla", I think, now.'

'Carmilla,' he said with pleasure.

'What are you doing in Cambridge?'

'I have come to see Provost Llewyllyn.'

This, he had decided, could be trotted out as the official reason for his visit.

'He is one of my father's oldest friends,' Marius went on, 'and I have not seen him for a very long time. Not since the Christening of his grandson, Tully Sarum, in the Chapel here three years ago.'

'You will find the Provost sadly changed.'

'I have also found Tully Sarum sadly changed.'

'You have been in Wiltshire? With my sister?' she asked, knowing the answer and the reason.

'I have been in Wiltshire with Theodosia.'

'A pleasant visit?'

'Marvellous. But far too short.'

'I see,' said Carmilla.

'Too short,' he said, 'and not likely to be repeated.'

'So having formed a taste for our . . . company, you have now come to me?' She laughed. 'You lovely little shit,' she said; 'you're as bad as Jeremy Morrison.'

'You liked Jeremy Morrison. He told me.'

'Did he now? Well, yes, I did like Jeremy Morrison. And I could like you very well, Marius Stern, you with your green eyes and your beautiful blond hair – '

' – Carmilla – ' he said, going towards her.

' – Were it not for one thing.'

There was a knock on the door. Entered a short, grizzled man with a short grizzled beard, dressed in a dark grey pin-stripe suit, an Old Etonian tie and beautifully polished black brogues.

'Richard,' said Carmilla to this man, 'here is Marius Stern, Gregory's boy. This,' she said to Marius, 'is Richard Harbinger. Your father published his books. The firm still does,' she said.

Richard Harbinger shook hands with Marius and kissed Carmilla sharply on the lips.

'Marius Stern,' he said to Marius, and 'Darling,' to Carmilla.

'Richard Harbinger, the explorer,' said Marius.

Harbinger preened, very slightly.

'I very much wish,' said Marius, 'that I could stay and talk to you. But I have an appointment with the Provost. So goodbye, sir. Goodbye . . . Miss Salinger.'

* * *

Well, thought Marius, as he walked round and behind Sitwell's Building and towards the Provost's Lodging, it was only a sixty-six to one shot, as Jeremy would say. I really had quite good value during the running; just for a moment I thought I was going to pull it off.

'Look, sweetheart,' said Len, the Provost's Private Secretary, when Marius had arrived at the Lodging and been shown into the withdrawing room, 'I *know* you very considerately rang up from London, and I *know* we agreed you could come here, but the old darling's had one of his turns, and I wouldn't want you to see him just now.'

'What's wrong with him?' Marius said.

'*Anno Domini*,' said Len. His tongue flicked like a lizard's between his long, thick lips.

'He is roughly my father's age. Not much more than fifty.'

'It takes people different ways, darling,' said Len: 'to some seventy is nothing, to others fifty is more than enough. A lot depends on what has been happening.'

'And what has been happening?'

'The elms in the College Avenue went rotten, for a start. He had to give the order to destroy them. And then his daughter Tullia – you know about her?'

Marius nodded.

'My cousin,' he said. 'Tullia, usually called Baby. Canteloupe's first wife, mother of Tullius called Sarum.'

'And there's another trouble for Tom. His grandson,

36

Tullius called Sarum. There have been . . . dismaying reports.'

'I don't wonder,' said Marius. 'I know all about *him*'

'One way and the other, duckie, you seem to know all about rather a lot.'

'All these people . . . are my connections,' said Marius.

Len giggled.

'You make yourself sound like a racehorse,' he said. 'They have connections, you know.'

'Yes,' said Marius, 'I do know. I was recently the connection of a racehorse. A very humble one, but nevertheless a connection.'

A dark and exceedingly pretty young man with a street arab's eyes and a pronounced limp came into the withdrawing room.

'The Provost will be all right for a while if you leave him to sleep,' said the young man to Len.

'How did you cope?'

'I sang him a Sicilian song, about how the tree nymphs are resigned to die peacefully with the trees.'

'Here is another connection for you,' said Len to Marius: 'Piero Caspar . . . Marius Stern,' he said to Piero.

Piero looked hard at Marius and said nothing.

'I suppose,' said Marius with commendable *savoir-faire*, 'that you were trying to comfort him about the elms in the College Avenue – singing that song? Mr Len has just been telling me about them. You must have gone to a lot of trouble to find exactly the right one.'

'Easy,' said Piero, who had now, it seemed, decided to accept Marius and favour him with speech. 'I made the song up. It consoled him slightly, as I said. But other things will be less easy. No song I can make up will console him, even slightly, for his daughter. The only

37

hope for Sir Tom,' he said to Len, 'will be summer and company. Lots of company.'

'"Tis company, villainous company, hath been his ruin,"' said Len, 'if one really cares to go into it.'

'*Good* company may be his restoration. Temporary at least.'

'But who is there to provide it?' said Len. 'Jeremy and Fielding are in the East. Gregory Stern is dead and his wife turned lesb – '

He pulled up out of respect for Marius.

'Say it,' said Marius. 'Lesbian. If only that was all. She has also turned feminist, leveller and a wretched screw about money. Luckily the lawyer has been one too many for her . . . so far. You know,' he said, not knowing why he said it, but obsurely feeling that Raisley Conyngham would wish him to grasp the opportunity offered, 'I know somebody who could be very good company for Sir Thomas later this summer. I have a friend at School: he is called Milo Hedley . . .'

'What was *he* doing here?' said Harbinger to Carmilla.

'Never mind him. Mind me.'

'*I* think he was sniffing.'

'What nonsense. He's far too young. Yes. Like that, Richard. More. More.'

'Don't let me find him here again. Arrogant little swine. So he'd have liked to stay and talk to me, would he? – but he had an appointment with the Provost.'

Carmilla, who knew that all this was passing because

Marius was tall (or soon would be) and fair, whereas Harbinger was stubby and swart, soothingly said:

'I haven't seen him for three years and don't expect to see him for another three. It's just that because his father was Gregory Stern we are both very large shareholders in the same firm. Salinger, Stern and Detterling, as it now is. I am on the board, and he will almost certainly be when he takes full control of his shares at his majority – not so very long now. So finding himself in Cambridge, he came to call on me – as a civility.'

'Let one civility be enough,' Harbinger said.

A funny old afternoon, thought Marius on the train back to London. It was a pity I couldn't see Sir Thomas; I'd tuned myself up for it. I wonder how ill he really is? That lame man, Caspar, seemed to think he was on the way out: 'No song I can make up will console him, even slightly, for his daughter.' His daughter Tullia, dead in Africa (of what?); my cousin; usually known as 'Baby'. Sir Thomas, of course, is my uncle by marriage with my mother's sister; but people don't refer to that very often because the poor lady is mad. I can hardly remember her, it is so long since she was put away. So Sir Tom is seldom 'Uncle Thomas', but usually 'Your father's old friend, Tom Llewyllyn'. Who is on the way out, Piero Caspar more or less said. But slowly. 'His best hope will be summer and company', something like that. I wonder if they'll take up my suggestion about Milo Hedley. That secretary man, Len, seemed interested. Perhaps they'd ask me as well. Why not? Anyway, I think Milo would like it: it would be a good introduction to Cambridge for him (though he isn't going to Lancaster), and he'd enjoy the atmosphere: he'd enjoy Len and Caspar. There's a distinction about them both, along with an air of mystery, as if there were always some intrigue going on, simmering away in the next room. It was typical that Caspar had made his song up. Not any old song off the peg, but one tailor-made for the meeting. I think Milo would enjoy that kind of a thing, and that Mr Conyngham would wish him to enjoy it.

Anyhow, Marius thought, I'll be seeing Milo tomorrow and I'll soon find out whether he would wish to keep the Provost company. Back to School tomorrow. Milo, Mr Conyngham; Tessa, Jakki; no 'Pally' Palairet any more. Pity I shall miss Rosie: her school, Collingham's in Kensington, doesn't start for another week, and she won't be back in London till the weekend. She'll miss both me and Tessa. And Jakki. Shall I ring up Tessa and ask her to travel down to Farncombe with me tomorrow? Or Jakki? Or both? No. Milo may meet me at Farncombe Station (if he and Mr Conyngham get back from Ullacote in time) and then it would be embarrassing, after everything that's happened.

And then he thought again of his dark sister, Rosie, whom he had not seen for many weeks, and of his mother, rangy Isobel, both of them in France, at St-Bertrand-de-Comminges, living in the chancel of a deconsecrated church; and he thought how twice that day (once with 'Young' John Groves and once with Len and Caspar) he had been nasty and disloyal about his mother, her parsimony or her love life (both, with Len and Caspar), and a tide of guilt and longing raced upon him, as he remembered how his mother used to crack her wicked jokes (before she was a socialist or a feminist) and kiss him on his ears and eyes. But she *has* grown mean, he told himself, and she *is* living as a lesbian, with Jean-Marie Guiscard's wife, Jo-Jo. Facts were facts and must be candidly acknowledged. Yet would she, he wondered, when they next met (and God alone knew when that would be), would she still kiss him on his ears and his eyes?

On the day that Rosie was due to leave St-Bertrand-de-Comminges for London, her mother, Isobel Stern, had an express letter from 'Young' John Groves.

'It's to tell me I need no longer pay the cook at the house in Chelsea,' she told Jo-Jo Guiscard, as they walked among the residual tombs beside the church which they inhabited.

'But I thought you'd stopped anyway.'

'Yes. Months ago.' Her normally fine-skinned and intelligent face became suddenly goose-pimpled and truculent. 'I don't mind that cook's being there to keep the place warm – convenient in case I had to go to London – but why should I pay him for doing nothing?'

'Because otherwise he might not stay,' said Jo-Jo, swivelling the strong waist between her springy hips so that she could look away across the tombs towards the foothills of the Pyrenees. 'He might go away and no longer keep the place warm for your convenience.'

'He knows when he's well off. But in any case the question no longer arises. "Other arrangements have been made," this letter says. I suspect that Marius has interfered. Who else? That young gentleman has got a few

41

nasty surprises coming to him – him and his fancy, independent ways.'

'What sort of nasty surprises? You can't stop his money. You can't even have it decreased. You've tried, and you've been seen off.'

'The sort of surprises,' said Isobel, 'which God keeps in reserve for pretty and conceited boys like Marius.'

Jo-Jo was starting to say that she didn't think Marius was conceited, though sometimes no doubt a bit difficult, as were all boys of his age, but she was interrupted by the arrival of Rosie Stern, who had by the hand Jo-Jo's two-and-a-half-year-old daughter, Oenone.

'We've been for our last walk on the ramparts,' said Oenone, and sniffed ominously. She pointed up to the walls above the churchyard. 'Up there,' she said; 'it's our favourite place to see the mountains. But now Rosie's going back to Looooondon – '

' – Stop whining like a little baby,' Rosie said, at the same time caressing Oenone's light brown hair with her free hand and bringing the child's head against her belly. 'I think my taxi should be here very soon. Shall I go and say goodbye to Jean-Marie?'

'I should leave him, darling,' said Jo-Jo; 'he's working, on his book. He's nearly at the end of it, and that makes him quite desperate to finish it up for good and get it out of the house. Interruptions will not be appreciated.'

'Say goodbye for me, then. Any messages for England?'

'Love to Marius,' said Jo-Jo.

'And try,' said Marius's mother, 'to encourage him to make some suitable arrangement for the summer holidays. He knows there's no room here. Perhaps he could go to this schoolmaster again – Braisley Cuntingham, or whatever he's called.'

Rosie shook her black tresses in reproof.

'Raisley Conyngham,' said Rosie earnestly, 'of Ullacote in the County of Somerset, Esquire. He trains racehorses. I looked him up in *Who's Who* and Burke's *Landed Gentry*.'

'And where did you discover *those* pernicious volumes?' said Isobel fiercely.

'Guilty,' said Jo-Jo. 'I brought 'em with me. One has to remind oneself, now one is a recluse and never sees one's old friends, of the correct style of addressing their envelopes.'

Isobel gave Jo-Jo a tough glance, but let this pass and reverted to Marius's pedagogue.

'Conyngham, then. He sounds a horrible reactionary pill, but so long as he'll take Master Marius off my hands I'll try to overlook it.'

'And can I please,' said Rosie, running one hand down the bony thigh which was covered by her tweed school skirt, 'have the cheque for Mrs Malcolm at Buttock's?'

'Here,' said Isobel rather too quickly; 'I've got it ready.'

She handed Rosie a folded cheque. Rosie opened it.

'You've forgotten to sign it,' Rosie said.

'Oh, have I? Well I haven't got a pen with me now. Tell Mrs Malcolm I'll send it on later.'

'I have a pen,' said Rosie. 'It will be easier – don't you think? – if you sign it now.'

Jo-Jo laughed. Isobel gritted her teeth and signed the cheque with Rosie's pen, using a stone coffin lid as a desk. An aggressive French car horn sounded from the track the other side of the church.

'I'll just get my case,' said Rosie, 'and go. Although it is important to say goodbye properly, it makes me nervous hanging about. So: God bless you, Oenone. We shall walk on the ramparts again in the summer.' She kissed the child on the forehead. 'Goodbye, Jo-Jo. I wish

Jean-Marie every success with his new book.' She shook hands firmly with Jo-Jo, like a guide mistress taking leave of an unreliable girl guide, whom, nevertheless, she was determined not to shame in front of the other girls by too deprecatory a gesture. 'And now, Mummy . . .' Her mother kissed her briefly on the lips.

'Au revoir, darling,' said Isobel: 'and love to that little brute, Marius – provided he clearly understands he's not to come here next holidays.'

'He doesn't in the least want to,' said Rosie in an absolutely neutral voice. 'I left my case ready on the sedilia in the sanctuary. Goodbye.'

'Extravagant little beast,' Isobel said, as Rosie disappeared round the apse; 'why couldn't she take a bus to the station at St-Gaudens?'

'Because she would have had to walk three miles to the bus stop with a heavy case. If you'd get that Lagonda of yours out of the garage, you could have given her a lift.'

'The Lagonda belongs to another world. When I was Rosie's age, Patricia and I would have walked three miles without even thinking of it, case or no case.'

'And look what's become of you both,' said Jo-Jo coarsely; 'Patricia in the loony bin for keepers, and you a middle-aged dyke that's come out of the closet in a hair shirt and sackcloth. Any old how, it's Rosie's money.'

'I know. I can't imagine why Gregory didn't leave *me* in charge of their allowances.'

'I think I can,' said Jo-Jo, and cackled with fond but malicious laughter.

* * *

In Hong Kong, two other people were discussing Marius, having been reminded of him by the sight of a string of racehorses which were being exercised on the maidan.

'You know,' said one-eyed pink-faced Fielding Gray, 'there was something terribly *fishy* about that job which Marius Stern had . . . as a groom in Raisley Conyngham's stable.'

'And God alone knows,' said Jeremy Morrison, 'what was going on at that race meeting at Bellhampton. I think Conyngham's charming chum, Milo Hedley, would have known – if I'd thought to ask.'

'You were too busy being buggered by him.'

'It wasn't that. I just didn't know there *was anything to ask about* – not until the rumpus began, and by then it was too late.'

'I think,' said Fielding, 'that we might do well to keep Marius away from Raisley Conyngham from now on.'

'But he'll be back at School by now – for the Cricket Quarter – right under Raisley's nose till the end of July.'

'What sort of beak was Conyngham when you were there?'

'That's four or five years ago now.' Jeremy twisted his huge round face in annoyance. He hated having to describe things. 'He was elegant,' he said at length, 'and he had style. Ironical, but seldom sarcastic. I *should* have been up to him for Latin and Greek verse in my last year, but he had a sabbatical. Without pay, they said. So I didn't get to know him as well as I would have done.'

'Did anyone see . . . anything odd in him . . . in those days?'

'No. Nor they don't see it now. He is, as far as I know, much respected as a wealthy and senior sort of beak who trains people up for Classical Schols at Oxford and Cambridge. He's had plenty of winners in *that* field.'

'I still don't think he's much good for Marius. I didn't think he was much good for him last holidays – and I think he'll be still less good for him if Marius joins him for the next.'

'Well now,' said Jeremy; 'I have given Marius a provisional invitation to join me, wherever I may be, at my expense, any time after the end of the quarter. So at least we can get him away from Conyngham by having him out as soon as it's over.'

'*If* Conyngham lets him come.'

'How can he stop him?'

'He's got the whole of next quarter to fix that. And if I'm not mistaken, your handsome friend, Milo Hedley, will be helping Conyngham to fix it. Where shall we be by the end of July?'

Jeremy made some mental calculations. Fielding watched the horses as they were walked by the grooms round the edge of the maidan, and thought of fair, slim Marius, dressed in his School tie and grey flannel suit, as he walked Lover Pie round the Paddock at Bellhampton.

'My gospel of oneness with the soil,' said Jeremy in a plausible and sympathetic voice, 'has had a good run of practice preaching here in Honkers. The humble like it because they think it lends them dignity – not that people work the soil in Honkers, but I've got some of 'em to feel what it might be if they did, and to favour the feeling. The commercial alligators also like the message, because they think it should do very well to keep the peasants (the producers of necessities) in their proper and docile place. So far, so good. But very soon now we must move back to Delhi for the beginning of the real show.'

'Have the Indians shown any interest?' said Fielding.

'You'd be surprised. They showed some when we last passed through, and a great deal more since we've been here and they've had a few days to think about it. My combination of primeval earth mysticism (discouraging riots and schism) with an implied promise of increased crops has got them wetting their dhotis at ministerial level. Whenever there is doubt as to my repute, my father's name turns the scale.'

'Shall we still be in India when Marius's Quarter ends? I don't think he'd care for it – all shit and beggars.'

'Late July . . . Probably not. By then we should be in Oz.'

'Don't tell me the Cobbers have fallen for primeval earth mysticism.'

'That kind of thing's in the air, Fielding. Everywhere. People want a bit of religion back in their lives. The established religions have failed them by turning into brassy bucket shops for cheap and violent left-wing ideas . . . whereas what the masses want is mystery, the numinous, sublimity – something to worship, to adore. The soil will do as well as anything else for that – *much better* than doped "freedom fighters" or ludicrous revolutionary antics.'

'Anyway, you'll write and ask Marius to join us as soon as the Quarter ends?'

'Happily. There *may* be a shift in the dates of our itinerary – but then we could switch his ticket accordingly. Why, Fielding, are you carrying on so much about Marius?'

'I just don't like what he's getting into with Raisley Conyngham. I think he's already in deeper than we know. That business with those horses at Bellhampton – it had the mark of some kind of rite, a rite of initiation or preparation.'

'What rubbish, my dear. How could you possibly know that? The thing is quite clear: Raisley Conyngham has a

47

fancy (certainly Platonic) for two bright favourites, Milo Hedley and Marius Stern, and the favourites have a fancy (perhaps *not* quite so Platonic) for each other; and so all three spent a month in the country, as happy as nabobs, in Raisley's swish Manor House, where, among other things, Marius could indulge his fondness for horses.'

'I hope you're right. And what was Tessa Malcolm doing in that gallery?'

'A pleasant and decorative addition to the party. Just as simple as that . . . though come to think of it, she did seem to be behaving rather strangely on the racecourse.'

'Exactly. *Everyone* was behaving rather strangely on that racecourse. I shall be very relieved when Marius joins us – *if* he joins us – in recognizable shape, in July. There's a very long time to go before then.'

So far from meeting Marius at Farncombe Station, Milo Hedley totally ignored him (as did Raisley Conyngham) for the first five days of the Quarter. Then, one afternoon, Hedley came and stood behind the net in which Marius was batting, and addressed him in the intervals between his strokes.

'So now you've had your little expedition to Wiltshire,' Milo said; 'how did it go?'

'Very agreeably, thank you.' Marius threw four balls back to the four bowlers. 'I think I've been in long enough,' he called.

'Oh no, you haven't,' said Milo: 'you stay there . . . Carry on for a bit,' he commanded the bowlers. 'And did you have a satisfied customer?' he asked Marius, as Marius squared up to the bowling.

The ball was a half-volley outside the off stump. Marius drove it off the front foot, easily and very hard, into the netting.

'There's a clever boy,' said Milo. 'Did you come up to scratch with her ladyship?'

'What do you know about that?'

'What Canteloupe's chum, Giles Glastonbury, told our own dear Raisley Conyngham. Or at least hinted. Canteloupe wants another son . . . so send for rorty little Marius the Egyptian.'

'I did my best,' said Marius. He hooked at a short ball and got a jagged bottom edge.

'Keep your eye on the thing,' said Milo.

'You're not making it easier.'

'How would you like to show me what happened between you and Lady Canteloupe . . . blow by blow? Strictly for the record? You needn't worry, Marius. I don't fancy you – you're the wrong shape and texture. It would be a "dry run", as soldiers say of a manoeuvre with blank cartridges: an academic exposition.'

'If you insist.'

Another short ball. This time he kept his eye on it and pulled it hard but far too high, clean out of the net.

'Not very kind, Marius. Now the bowler will have to fetch it. Let's have a little more consideration from you this afternoon. "If you insist," you say. That is not the spirit. The spirit is one of bland and blithe obedience. You know that. There is work ahead, Marius. Mr Conyngham and I are trying to prepare you for it, make you worthy of it. Let me not hear "If you insist" ever again.'

'All right. I'll show you, Milo. As soon as I'm done

with this net. Please stop putting me off,' Marius said, as he badly mistimed a square cut.

'Temper, temper. As it happens, I don't really want to know. Either she gets what she and Canteloupe want or she doesn't, and in the latter case you will, I suppose, be called on to try again. Lucky boy. Why did you leave Wiltshire early?'

'She was sick of the sight of me.'

Marius played forward and snicked what would have been an easy catch in the slips. 'If I go on playing so badly,' he said, 'I'll be kicked out of the Under Sixteen.'

'I do hope not, as that would seriously displease Mr Conyngham. He doesn't care for failure. So I'll leave you to concentrate on your pretty play – when you've told me what you got up to in Cambridge.'

'I looked round the place, paid a courtesy visit to Carmilla Salinger, who's on the board of our firm, Salinger, Stern and Detterling, met her friend, the explorer and author, Richard Harbinger, and then called on the Provost of Lancaster, as Mr Conyngham had suggested.'

Marius cut the ball very late and fine.

'There you are, you see,' said Milo, 'you can play beautifully if you don't upset yourself by being difficult and petulant, if you simply do what you are told and tell the truth. And what did the learned Provost say?'

'Nothing. He'd been taken ill. I spoke to some of his friends. They are worried about his condition, and want lots of company for him this summer. I don't quite know why, but I suggested you.'

'Me? He doesn't know me. I'm not even going to Lancaster . . . but do you know, little Marius, though *I* don't quite know why any more than you do, I think you have done a very good thing indeed. Though Mr Conyngham and I do not encourage action on impulse in normal circumstances, there *are* times when opportunities have to be recognized and swiftly taken. I think Conyngham will agree with me that you have done just that – spotted a valuable opportunity and snapped it up before it vanished. Well done, Marius the Egyptian.'

Marius glowed through his whole body. Milo's praise was nectar; the prospect of Raisley Conyngham's was ambrosia. He glanced the ball to left off the front foot, right off the leg stump in the perfect Prince Ranjhi manner.

'But let's not get too brilliant,' said Milo. '*That* sort of stroke is allowed only to people with an England cap. Still, as regards the Provost you have done well – though Raisley and I will want to hear a lot more about these friends of his whom you refer to.'

Although Rosie had not expected, or even much wanted, to see Tessa when she arrived back in London, she found Tessa still at her home in Buttock's Hotel, her departure for School having been delayed by a bout of colic. ('Overexcitement after all those goings on in Somerset,' said Maisie, not knowing anything about them.)

'I'm glad of an early chance to talk to you,' Tessa said to Rosie, as they walked in Hyde Park. 'Please understand that I'm now through with all of them.'

'All of whom?'

'Mr Conyngham. Milo Hedley. I'm free.'

Jakki Blessington, who, like Tessa, should normally have been back at their school by now, but had been kept at home by a plague of lice contracted on a recent visit to

51

Greece with her family, now met them, as had been arranged by telephone, under the pedestal of the Albert Memorial.

'Free of what?' Jakki enquired, having overheard the last words.

'I'm not quite sure of the answer to that,' said Tessa, 'but certainly of something one does well to be free of.'

She surveyed, with some distaste, the allegorical figures of Science, Industry and whatnot which were carved in relief on the pedestal.

'What about Marius in all this?' said Rosie anxiously.

'Marius is not free,' said Tessa. 'Infatuation has done its work. They have him.'

'Could you not help him to get away?'

'No. I knew that before I left them.'

'What are you going to do, then?' Jakki Blessington said.

'Be with you and Rosie again,' replied Tessa. 'Will you come with me tomorrow, Jakki? On the train back to School?'

'Oh, yes.'

'Last time we were on that train to Farncombe, I was horrid. I won't be now. And when I come back for the weekends, Rosie, all of me will come back here to you. The spirit as well as the flesh.'

'I could almost wish,' said Rosie, 'that some of you would stay at School with Marius and the rest, as it used to. What is to become of him now? Will nobody help him?'

'He does not wish to be helped. Before you can be saved from anything, you must wish to be saved.'

'How do you know,' said Rosie, 'that he does not wish to be saved?'

'I saw his face . . . when they took him away from the racecourse.'

'Racecourse?' said Rosie and Jakki.

So Tessa told them her story: how Marius, acting as groom to Raisley Conyngham's stallion Lover Pie, had been saved from riotous racehorses by Conyngham's head lass at Bellhampton racecourse a few weeks previously . . . while Tessa herself had been cruelly and squalidly betrayed amid the horseboxes; how Marius had been infatuated with his saviours, and she had fled clean away from her deceivers.

'. . . So he went with them,' she now said, 'and I took a train home. I wrote to Marius when I got to London, wrote to him at their house at Ullacote, begging him to leave them. He wrote back that I had missed the chance of a lifetime because of jealousy and disobedience. He said that we would not be seeing each other any more, and that at School, though we should always treat each other politely for the look of the thing, that would be all.'

'Oh dear,' said Rosie, 'oh dear, oh dear. But you will have Jakki at School at Farncombe, while I must stay here and go to Conyngham's all alone.'

'You'll be joining us in the autumn,' Jakki said, 'and for now you have my sister Caroline.'

'Caroline's a bit young to understand all this.'

'Your age,' said Jakki.

'My Jewish blood,' explained Rosie, 'makes me older and wiser.'

'It doesn't seem to have made Marius older and wiser.'

'Ātē,' said Rosie. 'Infatuation – the word Tessa used. Infatuation, ātē, "she that blindeth all", even, according to Homer, the King of the Gods himself. So what chance has Marius?'

* * *

In Wiltshire, Captain The Marquess Canteloupe and his Private Secretary, Leonard Percival, walked in the Rose Garden. Not fifty yards away from them the engines of Cant-Fun throbbed and sweated and belched poison in order to entertain the proletarians (and even some members of the middle class) who had paid £2.50 to enter the Multi-Dimensional and Trans-Galactic Travel Port (TAKE A SPACE-TIME CAPSULE TO THE END OF THE UNIVERSE); but in the Rose Garden, so skilfully had the abomination of Cant-Fun and its patrons been camouflaged and insulated, there was silence, except for the small and pleasant voices with which God's creatures celebrated the progress of the spring. Thus did the mills of Cant-Fun grind filth to extract the ore that would support a magnificent Marquisate; while my lord Marquess walked in his garden undisturbed. Undisturbed, that was, by sound or spectacle of Cant-Fun: he had other matters to mar his peace.

'Tullius,' he said to Leonard Percival now, 'commonly called Sarum. When and if we know that Theodosia is ripe, we shall have to think a lot about Tully.'

'We already have done. We have explored all the possibilities in our friend, La Soeur. La Soeur grows older and less daring. He wants to retire respectably; he is not prepared to jeopardize his considerable fortune by taking any further risks of the kind that amassed it. He will certainly take Tully into his keeping, for a very fat price: he will not procure his *quietus*, even for a fatter. So much for La Soeur. What about Daisy the nanny?'

'She loves the brat.'

'Like all nurses to small children, she doubtless has her dreams. "If there were dreams to sell," ' said Leonard, '"What would you buy? Some cost a passing bell . . ." Persuade that nurse that the most brilliant of her dreams is surely worth a passing bell – such a very small passing bell in this case: Tully's.'

'I can't risk it. If she chucked the offer back in my face, that would mean ruin. The lower classes,' said Canteloupe, 'love making drama of their integrity. We need somebody . . . who is too well conditioned to make a row even if he rejected the assignment. Someone who thinks rows are in bad taste – has better and more interesting things to do than make them. That's the trouble with people like this nurse: they have nothing much of interest to do – nothing to stop 'em making rows, in fact everything to encourage them, for rows mean that at least and at last they get a lot of attention.'

'There are surely other things which you can easily provide, things far more worth having than attention. Generous life cover, for example. If you were well served, Detterling, you would go as far as . . . generous life cover?'

'Of course.'

'Unrefusable, by any sensible person; and this nurse, Daisy, looks pretty sensible to me.'

'Yes. She also looks fundamentally decent. What we require is an act of fundamental indecency.'

'Well then, Detterling. You are a trained expert in the field.'

'Giles Glastonbury is another,' said Canteloupe, evading, at least for the time being, the implications of Percival's last remark. 'He advises approaching that schoolmaster, Raisley Conyngham. He is a man that understands this kind of predicament, Glastonbury says, does not take priggish moral views, and would be glad to be of service to . . . somebody like myself.'

'Then, why not let him be?'

'Any approach of this nature to Conyngham puts me in his power.'

'Not if he accepts,' said Leonard, 'as Glastonbury seems pretty sure he will do. He'll be as keen on secrecy as you are.'

'We should be in collusion, Leonard. I do not relish being in collusion with men like Raisley Conyngham.'

'You can't have it all your own way, Detterling. If you want your dirty work done for you, you can't expect lily-white hands in those that do it. It is absurd to be so fastidious.'

'You wouldn't take the thing on, I suppose?'

'No. I'm too close to it all. Just as you are, Detterling. You must see that.'

'I do,' said Canteloupe; 'that was desperation speaking.'

'Why not wait until her ladyship makes the happy announcement? After all,' said Leonard, 'she could be sterile for all we know, incapable of conceiving or bearing. Many women are. And in that case, there would be no point in . . . disposing . . . of Sarum, since there would be no other heir to replace him.'

'And why should there not be? If Theodosia is sterile, there are other women.'

'She adores you, Detterling. If you put her away, you'd break her heart.'

'What I must,' said Canteloupe, 'and what I will have, Leonard, is a satisfactory heir. It's no good your getting sentimental about Theodosia or anything else. As I have told you and others before, I want my dynasty to continue.'

'Not your dynasty, Detterling. A spurious one.'

'That is not what it will say in Burke.'

'Why does it matter to you what it says in Burke after you yourself are dead?'

'Because in such matters Burke states the truth. If Burke names my heir as the Marquess Canteloupe, then it is so.'

'If you will leave things be, Burke will name Tully as Canteloupe when you are gone. Why not settle for that?'

'Because Tully is not a proper human being, and will sire none. I simply want the thing to be *comme il faut*, Leonard.'

'But it isn't,' insisted Percival, stubborn as indeed he was paid to be. He was paid to find fault, to expose lies, to rip apart fraudulence . . . but at the very last to capitulate, to acquiesce, to reassure. This conversation, he reckoned, was about to reach the point when he must turn about and do that; but first, 'It isn't *comme il faut*,' said Leonard, 'and it never can be.'

'It can *appear* to be . . . and on the best authority.'

'Very well, if that is what you want. However, it seems you disdain the services of this versatile schoolmaster, highly recommended as they come, on some quirk of snobbery. Can you not persuade Glastonbury himself to oblige you in this little matter of Tully Sarum?'

'Glastonbury is a man of honour. He is permitted to *devise* dishonourable deeds, if his country or his friends have need of such, but not to take part in person. If only La Soeur hadn't turned into such a ghastly old woman . . .'

'No good bothering about him any more. Look, Detterling,' said Leonard. 'You are trying to devise a kind of hereditary tableau. The fact that it is not really hereditary does not make it any the less colourful or any the less splendid. So far, my blessing with thee. The snag is Sarum. Now then: Glastonbury, the expert, advises you

57

to approach this dominie, Conyngham. You demur, because you object to having such a man as an ally. This is nonsense. Men, even the greatest, that have played your game before you have always had men such as Conyngham (himself, after all, a gentleman) as allies. This is dead central to the tradition which you seek to preserve, Detterling – quite apart from being, as far as I can see, the only way of advancing your purpose. And in any case; surely you have already arranged to be introduced to Conyngham by Glastonbury?'

'The arrangement is provisional: I am committed to nothing.'

'Then if you want what you say you want, it is high time that you were.'

This was pretty much what Leonard was meant to say, at the end of such discussions, in ratification of the action proposed and desired by Canteloupe, who could then indulge himself with a few moral frills and furbelows, if he wanted to, before going on to follow the course agreed. On this occasion he said,

'I shall have to consult, not exactly my conscience, but my sense of fitness,' Canteloupe said. 'I think it will be satisfied if I can be sure that Tully's fate will somehow be worthy, worthy of his purported name and title.'

'You should have been in show-biz,' Leonard remarked, for he could not resist it; 'you are a natural ringmaster.'

This was *not* what Leonard was meant to say, either at the end of these exchanges or indeed at any other stage of them. Not only was he meant to conclude strictly on a note of reassurance, he was meant to persist in taking the whole affair seriously, a requirement which precluded observations of the kind he had just made. In this instance, however, Canteloupe seemed inclined to over-look the misdemeanour, possibly because the unexpected appearance of Theodosia (who seldom came within a furlong of Leonard Percival unless there was no help for it) now claimed his attention.

'Today,' said Raisley Conyngham, 'we will only gossip.'

Conyngham, Marius and Milo Hedley walked on the Terrace above Green, where a First XI Trial was being played. Milo Hedley, a very fair cricketer who had deserted the game for lawn tennis, had no part in this Trial; nor had Marius, who was too young. Conyngham, who was too old and for many other reasons disqualified, was wearing, rather oddly, long white trousers and a Free Forester blazer. Such kit, on his spare figure, made him resemble a cox who had been carefully chosen not to inspire amatory notions in the oarsmen.

'I am not a cricketer,' Conyngham had explained when Milo and Marius called for him at his chambers, 'but I am what is known as Founder's Kin, and was therefore elected to the Foresters automatically at the age of eighteen. Since the blazer is quite decorative, I like to give it an airing from time to time.'

And now, on the terrace, 'The form our gossip will take is this,' he said. 'Let us consider what advantage would accrue if Milo were in fact invited to spend some part of the late summer with Provost Llewyllyn of Lancaster.'

'A pleasant introduction to Cambridge,' said Milo, 'though Lancaster is not my college. I have always heard that the long vac is a time for leisurely reading while the university, one quarter full, drowses around one.'

'That was the case forty years ago,' said Raisley. 'Now there is a full-blown Festival of every kind of cultural rubbish in the almanack, and the whole place is heaving with Americans terrified of being fleeced of twopence and swaggering nigger trash.'

'I don't suppose,' said Marius, 'that either will be allowed in the Provost's Lodging.'

'But both will be allowed into the College at large. And some of the artistes and conferenciers and creative personalities or whomever will certainly be billeted there. I understand that this year there is to be a Soul Festival running parallel with the other one.'

Raisley Conyngham shuddered. Milo Hedley patted his helmet haircut (Greek Archaic style), scowled at Raisley for shattering his Edwardian dream of Cambridge in the long vacation, and smiled his *kouros* smile at Marius, who simpered foxily back.

'The point is,' said Milo, 'that I should get to know the Provost. That has to be a good thing.'

'Why?' said Raisley. 'I hear Sir Thomas is visibly declining – he was too ill to see Marius, we recall. I also hear that his intellects are disturbed. Winstanley writes that he has been mentally unbalanced ever since the elms in the College Avenue had to be destroyed.'

'Apart from other dons whom Milo might meet,' said Marius, 'there are two figures of interest. The Provost's Private Secretary, Len, and – '

'"Len" what?'

'He never told me. "Hallo, darling, I'm the Provost's Secretary," he said; "you call me Len." But though he talks like that, he isn't at all camp. In fact he's very tough. And virile. His dress is so vulgar – mauve shoes with a blood-orange tie – that it hits you in the face like a hammer, and is obviously meant to.'

An aspirant to the First XI was clumsily caught at the wicket. Raisley applauded with delicate aplomb.

'What is the point of this Len person?' he said.

'He seems to run the College in the Provost's name. Just before I left – after he'd taken down Milo's full name and address, so that he could be called on "at a need", said he, to amuse the Provost – just before I left,' Marius said, 'there was a telephone call. It was the police, to say that they suspected one of the Lancaster undergraduates of pushing cocaine. He'd taken refuge inside the College, where they had no powers of entry or arrest without the permission of the Provost, who is Sovereign on College Grounds – quite apart from being, as Fielding Gray once told me, the Avatar of the Founder, the Blessed King Henry VI.

'"Right, darling," said Len on the telephone to the police: "the Provost is too ill to be consulted. I have his seal and his delegated *Jus Judicis* – in other words, I'm boss of the circus. Now it's no good your coming in here in broad daylight and asking for this nasty little junk artist – even if I give permission – because all the beastly lower-class students would start shouting 'Fascist' and tear you and your lovely constables to pieces. And that would upset the College peacocks. On the other hand, if I expel him from the College, so that you could get him as he comes out, he would probably just refuse to budge. So what we do is, we give you a key to the postern gate, you come in at two in the morning, and I will meet you and guide you to the young man's rooms . . . where you prick him with something to keep him quiet and carry him out of here for ever, but I mean for ever, darling, and no one any the wiser about how it all happened. *Just see that your charges stick.* I shall come to your station at four-thirty this afternoon, and there we can arrange details . . ."

"And jolly good riddance," Len said to me, "that's one more of these dope pests out of the way."'

Milo, whose elder brother had died of heroin, approved of this story.

'It's not only that they're pests,' he said; 'they're so bloody boring. All they can talk about is their habit and how to supply it.'

'So,' said Raisley Conyngham, as they turned at the Chapel end of the Terrace and began the countermarch, 'one senses, Milo, that "Len" will be to your taste. Who,' he said to Marius, 'was the second personality of your visit?'

'An Italian undergraduate called Piero Caspar. I knew him by repute,' said Marius, 'even before I met him. He was secretary to Ptolemaeos Tunne, who is the uncle of a girl called Jo-Jo Pelham, who married a Frenchman called Guiscard but then became attached to my mother.'

'Ah,' said Raisley Conyngham, in benign acceptance of all this.

'Ptolemaeos is now dead. Caspar has inherited much of his money and the College most of the rest. Caspar is in his third year at Lancaster, and Len says they hope to make him a Fellow. In fact, "We *shall* make him a Fellow," Len said, after Caspar had gone and he was taking me to the Main Gate to get a taxi.'

'Very civil of him. But how did you come to meet this Caspar in the first place? What was *he* doing in the Provost's Lodging?'

'He'd been with the Provost, singing a Sicilian song to him. After which he came downstairs from the Provost's bedroom to report to Len about what effect it had had. Apparently it wasn't *really* a Sicilian song because Caspar had made it up. Mind you, Caspar isn't Caspar's real name, but only the name by which Ptolemaeos Tunne adopted him after he escaped from a monastery near Venice.'

'I apprehend,' said Raisley Conyngham,' that all that will bear a little investigation. Meanwhile, Marius, did you gather what the song was about?'

'About tree nymphs. How they are resigned to die when their trees die.'

'I see,' said Raisley Conyngham; 'all this because Sir Thomas is still obsessed by the dead elms of Lancaster. It sounds as if they'll be the end of him. I think,' he said to Milo, 'that a study of Len and Piero Caspar – to say nothing of what's left of the Provost – might pass an interesting month this summer.'

'I'll think about it,' Milo said.

'I thought you thought it was such a good idea,' said Marius.

'I've had second thoughts.' Milo looked at Raisley Conyngham in a challenging manner. 'I'm leaving here at the end of this quarter,' he said. 'I'm going to a new world. I must decide for myself on the best manner of my entering it. I'm not sure, after all, that Lancaster in the long vacation is the best way.'

Marius looked carefully at Conyngham, to see how he was reacting to this disobedience. Raisley's face had simply gone blank. At first Marius thought: He can't cope. Milo is grown too big for him. But when Raisley Conyngham said, 'Suit yourself, Milo; I think that they'd be just as glad to have Marius as you,' Marius saw that Milo was sagging all down his body like a ripped garbage bag. Milo thought he was a big boy at long last, Marius conjectured. He wanted to go and stay at Lancaster, he wanted to have his way and go there, *as if by his own decision*. He was therefore annoyed with Mr Conyngham for contradicting him at the beginning of the discussion and for simply taking him for granted at the end of it. Milo, in a word, was in a pet, and was now about to be put in his place. And quite right too, Marius thought. When it comes to the marrow of the thing, Milo couldn't do without Mr Conyngham any more than I could. Mr Conyngham . . . is creating us.

'I only meant,' said Milo, trying to save face, 'that the matter should be fully discussed before any decisions are made.'

'It has been,' said Raisley, 'and they have been. After due cogitation, it has been decided that you should go to the Provost's Lodging this summer – if he is still alive and if you are called for.'

'And what will Marius do this summer?' said Milo, still blustering slightly.

Raisley dowsed the last sparks of rebellion by taking up Milo's question but utterly ignoring Milo.

'Your mother won't want you in France?' said Raisley to Marius.

'I think not. Can I come to Ullacote?'

'No,' said Raisley. 'You and Jenny would seek each other out. You understand that I can't have that. Any attempt, on the part of either of you, to renew the magic which I made for you at Bellhampton would destroy it utterly now. But do not look so sad, little Marius the Egyptian. There will be something . . . to help you pass the long, hot summer. I promise you that.'

* * *

In the repaired romanesque chancel, under the ramparts of St-Bertrand-de-Comminges, Isobel Stern lay in bed with Jo-Jo Guiscard, both panting slightly, having taken their fill of honey-sweet love.

'Thank God Rosie's gone,' said Isobel at last.

'But she's a dear girl. And so sweet with Oenone.'

'So intense,' Isobel said. 'Those great black eyes, under that huge expanse of white marble forehead, under those masses of raven hair. So different from Marius. I wish Marius didn't dislike me so much these days. When he was younger . . . we were almost lovers in a way.'

'I've always said that sons would make the best lovers. It's not too late for you and Marius,' Jo-Jo said, 'only he don't like your infernal meanness about money. Nor I don't, neither. We've all got plenty, one way and the other. Let's make the most of it.'

'In a world so full of misery – ' Isobel began her habitual sermon –

' – There's no cause to add one's own to it,' Jo-Jo interrupted with her habitual confutation. 'If you want to do something about the misery, then give some of your money away in good causes. But you don't do that. You just moan about the guilt of having it and lock it up tighter and tighter. Oenone will be sad,' she said, firmly changing the subject, as she knew by now that Isobel's stinginess was pathological, like that of the great Dickensian misers, and there was no longer any point in attempting rational discussion of it, 'now that Rosie's gone.'

'I shall care for her,' said Isobel, 'and so will her father.'

'So shall not I,' said Jo-Jo. 'Now, if she'd been my son, it might have been a very different matter. But as it is, we're best apart, Oenone and I. The way she looks at me, she thinks I'm a rather nasty joke. Come to that, I think pretty much the same of her.'

'She's clever,' said Isobel. 'Soon she must begin to be educated. We must find the right school. I suppose Jean-Marie will know about the French ones?'

'An English one, I *think*, darling,' Jo-Jo said; 'get her nicely out of the way for three months at a time.'

'Leave aside,' said Isobel, 'that English boarding schools cost intolerable sums of money and are repulsive instances of privilege, you must realize that these days you cannot get your child out of the way, not in any of 'em, not for anything near three months – not any more. Three *weeks*, if you're lucky. They now have fortnightly exeats, special parents' weekends, and a half-term holiday as long as the Boat Race. The whole thing's a nightmare, to judge from Marius's prep school.'

'Can't you just *pay* the school to keep them,' said Jo-Jo, 'during all those exeats and things? That's what boarding schools are for – to stop them from being a nuisance.'

'They don't quite see it like that any more. The last school I knew of,' said Isobel, 'that provided the sort of Squeersian service you seem to be after, was where poor Baby was sent in 1973. To be strictly fair, it was jolly good in its way. Work, games, discipline – all tophole, as the headmistress, Miss Wentworth Rex, would have said. And the children were hardly let out at all. Baby adored it – she was at a very competitive stage. And we all know how Baby wound up.'

'I'll tell you a thing,' said Jo-Jo, full of loyalty to her dead friend and spite towards the living one, 'Baby was fifty times as exciting as you. *You* are like an animated statue lying on top of one, a kind of female missionary, if you take my meaning, durable and serviceable, indeed, but without a hint of invention or variation. Baby was like a soft and sensitive snake, coiling and licking and flicking all round one's body. What was that school called? The one she went to in '73?'

'Radigund's,' said Isobel huffily, 'after the Queen of the Amazons.'

'Does it still exist?'

'No doubt. It was very well found for what it was. When Baby left it, she could quote you half the *Iliad* – in Greek.'

'I wonder she never went on to Oxford or Cambridge.'

'Too keen to marry Canteloupe. And bored stiff, I should think, with learning all that Greek poetry by rote.'

'If you don't get poetry by heart at that age,' said Jo-Jo, 'you never will. I wish I had. That's one thing I can give Oenone – a proper education, with a store of poetry she's learned by heart.'

'By rote.'

'It's what he'd learned by rote at school that kept Robert Kee sane for four years in a prisoner-of-war camp. He wrote it all out and studied it afresh, like a text. I want Oenone to be like that. Not only must she have Greek, but she must have the other things Kee had – discipline and *rule*. Rule is the basis of all intellectual achievement – and of all Art.'

'Aren't you leaving people out?' sniffed Isobel. '*People* are more important, you know, than Intellect or Art.'

'Without Intellect and Art they are hardly people. Certainly not people worth any sort of consideration. Art is the only thing that keeps us human,' Jo-Jo said. 'If Radigund's, as well as keeping Oenone out of the way, can teach her the Rule that underlies Art,' she said, 'then Oenone will have had the finest gift of all, and I shall no longer feel guilty and squalid, like a pair of wet knickers, whenever I look at her. I shall ring up Radigund's tomorrow. Uncle Ptolemaeos,' she carolled, 'will find me the address and the number. Perhaps he'll fix it all for me.'

'Oenone is not yet three, darling. And Ptolemaeos is dead.'

'So he is.' She rested her head on Isobel's long breasts. 'A statue,' she said, 'but a lovely statue: warm marble. Well, we can soon find out about Radigund's,' she giggled, 'and book Oenone in against she's old enough, through "Young" John Groves, the lawyer.'

'Of course,' said the headmaster, Percy de la Poeur Chevenix, as they took their seats on the boundary of Green, 'we make a good deal less of this than you did in your time, I dare say.'

Canteloupe and Giles Glastonbury had come to Canteloupe's old School near Farncombe to watch the First XI play I Zingari. Later in the afternoon, Glastonbury was to introduce Canteloupe to Raisley Conyngham, a rendezvous having been arranged for the tea interval. But meanwhile the plan for the first part of the afternoon had been badly upset: the headmaster, who had *not* been told (why should he be?) that Canteloupe was coming, nevertheless spotted him and recognized him, from one of his photographs in the press, soon after his arrival, and insisted on giving him, as a prominent Old Boy, a personally guided tour of all the recent additions to the School – the Ceramists' Centre (bulging jugs), the Summerskill Library (pamphlets about welfare benefits, venereal diseases and the wickedness of manly diversions), the 2000 Careers' Bureau (advice on how to enter the 'creative' and 'caring' professions), and the Medical and Psychiatric Complex, which was, as Glastonbury had proclaimed in a moment of mutiny, a malingerers' paradise, with huge posters advertising all the illnesses you could claim to be suffering from if you were too stupid to think of any for yourself.

'It is important that the young should be clinically aware,' intoned the headmaster, 'of every aspect of forensic or domestic medication.'

At this juncture, while tottering out towards the next edifying exhibit, Canteloupe and Glastonbury had been rescued by a very old, stylish and voluminous gentleman, who was demanding and not getting a Beecham's powder, this sort of thing being too unsophisticated to be comprised in forensic or domestic medication.

'Ah, *Detterling*,' said the voluminous old gentleman (voluminous in the full sense, meaning both loose and ample); 'the only boy that ever made a double century in a School Match.'

'Good afternoon, Senior Usher,' said Canteloupe, as if addressing the Queen Mother in male drag; 'this is my friend, Giles Glastonbury,' and then to Glastonbury: 'the Senior Usher of the School.'

The headmaster's face twisted with distaste while this introduction went on.

'I was the last of the Senior Ushers,' explained the Senior Usher to Glastonbury, 'so they let me keep the title when I retired a generation ago. They also let me hang around the place and make myself useful. Occasional lectures, that kind of thing.' And then, to a white-coated attendant, 'No, I need neither "upping" nor "downing": simply a Beecham's powder for a mild headache.'

The attendant produced an enormous octagonal pill which the Senior Usher waved away.

'Time to be getting on,' said the headmaster, 'to the Personal Relations Laboratory.'

'Detterling don't want that rubbish,' said the Senior Usher, 'he wants the cricket. Right, Detterling?'

'Right,' said Canteloupe.

So to the cricket they had gone at last, the headmaster still in rather spiky attendance on Canteloupe, and the Senior Usher recalling ball by ball, for Giles's benefit, Canteloupe's celebrated double century of nearly half a century before. And then, as they sat down on a bench just under the Terrace,

'Of course,' said the headmaster, 'we make a good deal less of this than you did in your time, I dare say.'

'Do you indeed, headmaster?' Canteloupe said. 'No doubt you have so many things more worth the doing.'

'We rather think we do,' simpered La Poeur Chevenix.

'Such as?'

'All the arts and activities which I have just been showing you.'

'To say nothing of the Personal Relations Laboratory, which we missed. We also missed the Armoury, I think?'

'We no longer have one. There is a hut where those that wish may fire airguns under the supervision of a visiting corporal, who comes over from Aldershot once a fortnight.' The headmaster rose with an air of having scored. 'You'll excuse me, Canteloupe,' he said, in a Kentish-urban whine. 'I'm due at the Precinct of Drama to attend a rehearsal of Edward Bond's new masterpiece.'

'It may surprise you to know,' said the Senior Usher, as the headmaster lurched self-importantly away, picking at his fingernails, 'that he's a genuine La Poeur Chevenix. He puts the accent on, you know.'

'What would one have found,' enquired Glastonbury, 'at the Personal Relations Library?'

'At the moment they're very keen, I believe, on what they call "odour compatibility",' said the Senior Usher. 'Two people go into a small enclosed space together and fart. If they like, or can at least tolerate, the smell of each other's farts, then a "Life Union" is pronounced feasible, if not obligatory. That kind of thing.'

'I wonder the old place keeps going at all,' said Canteloupe; 'but this lot seem quite sharp in the field . . . Good man,' he called as the bowler caught a hissing return to his wide left hand from I Zingari's No. 4.

'It's quite simple,' said the Senior Usher; 'all those flops, weeds and wrecks who made a grizzling nuisance of themselves in your day and mine now go and suppurate together in those new centres or complexes or whatever. This leaves the decent fellows free to get on without disruption or interference. So you see, all this new non-sense has paid off because it gets the junk out of the way. Though I don't think La Poeur Chevenix would put it quite like that.'

'He didn't seem enchanted with *you*.'

'But he's stuck with me. I have a special redundancy contract, arranged and subsidized by grateful Old Boys, with the assistance of the then headmaster, in 1955. I don't go,' gloated the old man, 'till they carry me out in my box.'

'Yes,' said Canteloupe sourly, 'I remember the sub-scription list coming round.'

'I won't ask you what you subscribed. Do you ever see Fielding Gray these days? I found out, on the q.t., that he put up rather a lot.'

'Fielding was always extravagant. If you won't think me impertinent, sir,' Canteloupe said, 'we always had the

71

impression . . . that you had extensive private means. Where, then, was the necessity of the subscription?'

'My dear boy, there was no necessity, it was an act of homage. I was the last Senior Usher. The abolition of this ancient and honourable office could not pass without proper remark, of which I was the beneficiary.'

'Why on earth,' said Glastonbury, 'was the post abolished?'

'Because as long as there was a "Senior Usher", all the rest of the staff were obviously also "ushers" – and they didn't care for the title. Sounded too like an upper servant . . . which historically, of course, is exactly what school-masters are: upper servants to the nobility and gentry. Why try to disguise the fact?'

The players drifted off the field.

'Come and have tea,' said the Senior Usher; 'we can have it with the players.'

Just for a moment, as he thought of the pavilion with its names and yellow photographs and smell of linseed oil, Canteloupe's nostrils twitched with longing. Glastonbury gave him a good sharp nudge.

'Sorry, sir,' said Canteloupe to the Senior Usher; 'we're due elsewhere.'

'Elsewhere' was the Chapel, where they were to meet Raisley Conyngham at four-thirty in the Narthex, 'a cool and passably elegant *venue*,' as Raisley had observed to Glastonbury on the telephone.

With Raisley was Milo Hedley. When he saw the eyes

of both Canteloupe and Glastonbury flicker with annoyance, Raisley said:

'You must not mind his presence. Milo Hedley is my memory. And my lieutenant. Milo, this is Lord Canteloupe, of whom you will have heard, and his friend Major Glastonbury, whom you have already met at Ullacote.'

'Good afternoon, gentlemen,' Milo said.

As he came forward to shake hands, he revealed the 1939–45 Memorial Screen, which until now he had been masking. And then, 'What have we here?' said Canteloupe, making towards the screen and inspecting the triple ranks of the dead. '"Connaught la Poeur Beresford, the Irish Guards." Killed at Anzio, or was it Salerno? But let us bate that question, as this memorial poses others of greater moment.

'For I remember a service that was held in this Chapel very soon after the war in Europe ended. The Senior Usher read out the names of the fallen. (Alastair Edward Farquar Morrison, Victoria Cross, the Norfolk Yeomanry: elder brother of Peter Morrison, that is now called Luffham of Whereham.) And then the headmaster of the day gave a very striking sermon, not popular at the time, but which I have remembered, ever since, for its charity and truth. Not, you understand, that charity and truth are necessarily much in my line, but they are qualities which, one way or the other, impress. The headmaster said that there was no going back to the old life which we had led before the war because the enormity of what had occurred was too great to be ignored, and henceforth all our efforts would be required for its purification. (Lancelot Sassoon-Warburton, Ninth Lancers: I rather think he won the Grand Military, just before the war, up on his own horse, Lauderdale.)

'We were angry with the headmaster that afternoon,

myself and others, because we knew that the evil, the enormity of which he spoke, was none of our making, and we wanted – we were surely entitled to – reparations for the misery of the last five years, reparations from those that were guilty . . . rightful bounty, to us, as rightful conquerors. So although I always remembered and theoretically admired the head man's moral sermon, given on the Sunday just after the war, I also thought, as we all thought over the years, that I had been cheated: I had not been accorded a warrior's prizes; I had been blamed, or at least harassed and discommoded without restitution, because of an evil which others – the Germans – had set in motion. (The Honourable Andrew Usquebaugh, Midshipman, the Royal Navy.)

'So what in the end had we been fighting for? Not for ourselves, nor for our country as we wanted it to be, but for somebody else's conception of our country as his conception of duty would order it. We had been fighting, in a word, for the headmaster, that he might survive in safety to hector and lecture us in the name of morality. So we ceased to play a straight and open game, as we had used to play, because those that did so were from now on and for ever to be sanctimoniously pestered, by the headmaster and others far worse. We began to play little private games instead . . . out of the way, where the headmaster and the rest could not get at us or at our gains. Disallowed the rewards we had won honestly, we recouped by dishonesty: by fraud or deceit or sharp practice we made for ourselves little glades or oases of private wealth and pleasure . . . only to find, of course, that even here we were interfered with, by ill chance or the malice of God. (Geoffrey Alaric Williams, the King's Shropshire Light Infantry.) I myself, granted a great inheritance, could not, of course, render it entirely private. But I was able to indulge certain private plans for it, who should have it after me and how he should enjoy it. I was able to defy (up to a point) regulation and prohibition, the interference of the headmaster and his agents, until I had the thing shaped as I liked it.

'*That's* the kind of thing that *I* had been fighting for,' said Canteloupe, slapping the palm of his right hand on to the marble of the 1939–45 Memorial Screen.

'You never fought at all,' said Glastonbury; 'you never heard a shot fired closer than three miles away.'

'I helped you with your dirty work in Delhi,' said Canteloupe, 'dirty work that had to be done for King and Emperor. That was contribution enough.'

'Gentlemen, gentlemen,' said Raisley Conyngham. 'You were saying,' he said to Canteloupe, 'that despite the moral pronouncement and striving of the former "headmaster" and his like, you had managed to proceed effectively in private, "until you had the thing shaped as you liked it". Am I to understand that this state of affairs still obtains – or not?'

'The general shape is still well enough. One particular element is faulty. It will be replaced, but there will still be a problem.'

'Be plain,' said Glastonbury. 'Conyngham is a man of the world, as you are. He will pardon your long exordium' – Glastonbury pointed at the 1939–45 Memorial Screen – 'if only for its historical interest, but the time has come to declare yourself. This boy,' Glastonbury said to Raisley Conyngham and pointed at Milo Hedley, 'you're sure he's to be trusted? He was slinking about in rather a sinister way at that race meeting at Bellhampton.'

'He was obeying the orders I had given him.'

'Very well,' said Glastonbury. 'What Canteloupe wants

75

to tell you is that his heir, Lord Sarum of Old Sarum, is unsound. He can see his way to procuring a new one – '

' – Ah,' interrupted Raisley; 'my surmise was correct. That was what was wanted from Marius. Has he done his duty?'

'I think so,' said Canteloupe, thinking of what Thea had said, heedless of Leonard Percival, when she had come to them in the Rose Garden: 'I think so,' he said, 'unless Lady Canteloupe is much mistaken. Is Marius anywhere around, by the way? I have an unwise desire to thank him. Perhaps a tip would be in order.'

'Marius is playing cricket for the School Under Sixteen XI,' said Milo Hedley, 'at Christ's Hospital.'

'Not available, then. Just as well, I dare say. Though it is some time since I have seen him, and I should have liked another look at his father's son.'

'And at your own son's father?' said Milo Hedley.

'Tut, Milo,' said Raisley Conyngham. 'But if things come about as Milo indicates,' he said to Canteloupe, 'if Lady Canteloupe is with child, and if the child is male, and if there are no unfortunate complications of the kind that have affected Lord Sarum, then your problem is well on the way to being solved.'

'A lot of "ifs",' said Canteloupe. 'And even if they all run my way, there is *still* a problem.'

'Oh yes?' said Raisley.

'You must know what it is.'

'I must hear you say it, if only in order to be certain.'

Canteloupe turned to the 1939–45 Memorial.

'"Alastair Edward Farquar Morrison",' he read. 'He was killed outright, leaving his younger brother, Peter, undisputed heir to the family estates. No problem there. Peter himself has two sons: Jeremy, the younger, who is quick; Nickie, the elder, who is as good as dead. But not quite dead. Mad, in St Bede's Asylum. Luckily, in the case of the Morrisons the entail provides that if the eldest son is a lunatic or similarly incapacitated he can be set aside, while the rights under the entail escheat to the next in line. So there is no real problem there either. But there would be, if Peter's barony were a proper and heritable one instead of a squalid life peerage. *If* the barony could be inherited at Peter's death, it would be inherited by poor Nickie in St Bede's, whose brain has rotted in his head. Now, my title, my Marquisate, *can* be inherited and *must* go to the first-born son. Do I make myself plain now?'

'Yes,' said Raisley; 'but pray be direct. If, as I apprehend, you want my assistance, you must say the thing direct.'

'Very well. Tullius, whom Glastonbury calls Sarum of Old Sarum, must soon be gone, in order to give his place, all of his place, to the new heir. He must not be put under care at St Bede's or in La Soeur's Nursing Home – '

' – Ah,' said Raisley, 'I wondered how soon *his* name would crop up – '

' – He must be gone, quite gone. He must have, of course, a kindly going of it . . . if possible one worthy of his present situation. He must have a going which can be suitably recorded by a noble or at least distinguished monument. Have I said what you wish to hear?'

'Yes,' said Raisley Conyngham. 'There is a neat and ironic solution. Tell them, Milo.'

'Marius,' Milo said. 'Marius giveth, and Marius taketh away.'

'We had a little rule in India,' said Glastonbury, 'that we didn't use children.'

'Things have moved on since then,' Milo said.

'But why is Marius particularly suitable for this task?'

'Because Marius is under an oath, or at any rate a bond, of obedience,' Raisley Conyngham said; 'he has dedicated himself, and has had that dedication confirmed by a laying on of hands.'

'What sort of talk is this?' said Glastonbury.

'The truth,' said Milo. 'We had the two of them, Tessa Malcolm and Marius Stern. Tessa, Teresa, escaped us, partly because of my.clumsiness. But with Marius we did not fail. He is, as Mr Conyngham observes, dedicated – dedicated beyond any possible apostasy.'

'I think it most damnably repulsive,' said Glastonbury, like an old prostitute righteously railing against child molesters, 'that a mere boy should be involved.'

'Yet you can countenance the removal of a mere infant?'

'The infant is spoilt, tainted, mentally deformed.'

'It is at least possible,' said Raisley, 'that Marius is spoilt, tainted, mentally deformed. Otherwise we might not have been able to hold him. Teresa Malcolm got away from us easily enough: when she smelt something wrong, she walked straight out. A healthy, normal girl. Now, I agree that Marius looks healthy and normal enough, indeed outstandingly so. Why, then, did he stay with us, *after* he had had revealed to him just such things as put Teresa instantly to flight? Well, let us not forget that he has a very dubious mental heritage, and that he nearly killed one of his schoolfellows in a fit of fury. And so, my dear Glastonbury, we can plausibly claim that we are not sowing evil in the breast of an innocent child, but merely evoking what is already there . . . conjuring the demon in the demi-god, Marius the Egyptian.'

'Canteloupe says he wants a kindly end for Sarum. Can this "demon" provide it?'

'If so instructed,' said Raisley Conyngham. 'Certain

types of demon – incubi and succubi, for example – are notorious for their kindness.'

'I wonder how Marius is getting on with the Under Sixteen at Christ's Hospital,' said Jakki to Tessa, as they stood on the terrace watching the First XI bat against I Zingari.

'I wish they hadn't cancelled the Girls' Under Sixteen against Benenden,' said Tessa. 'My big chance, with Hattie Rogers out of the way in Big San. Twenty or thirty runs, or a couple of wickets, and I'd have been in the side for good.'

'Why did they cancel?' said Jakki.

'Someone's disgusting junkie brother fell down dead on a visit. The day before yesterday. Proper respect must be paid, they said – after all, he *was* called Lord Ferdinand something. God, how right Milo Hedley always was about all that – junkies are nothing but a boring bloody nuisance.'

'So are all ill people, come to that,' said Jakki.

They both considered this indisputable comment in silence. A shambling figure, which for some time had been making its way round the ground from the pavilion, started up the steps on to the Terrace.

'The Senior Usher,' Jakki said. 'I hope he'll do his Art Lectures again this winter.'

The figure tripped, stumbled and fell sprawled across the steps.

'Come on, girl,' said Tessa.

They ran to the old man on the steps, and after considerable effort got him to his feet.

'Thank you, ladies,' muttered the Senior Usher, his mouth oddly twisted; 'pray bring me to the Chapel.'

'It's a good hundred yards along the Terrace, sir. Hadn't we better – '

' – Bring me to the Narthex of the Chapel.'

'The Narthex?' said Tessa.

'West end,' said Jakki, 'the bit before the Nave begins.'

'You see,' mumbled the Senior Usher, 'I must read the names once more.'

But now, the girls were thankful to see, he made no effort to move further up the steps or on to the Terrace.

'"Connaught la Poeur Beresford," he said, '"the Irish Guards. Michael John Blood, the Royal Corps of Signals. Tobias Ainsworth Jackson, the Royal Army Ordnance Corps."'

The old man took a deep breath. '"Alastair Edward Farquar Morrison, Victoria Cross, the Norfolk Yeomanry."'

Slowly the Senior Usher sank to his knees, while the two girls contrived to support him on either side.

'"Morgan Waldo, Seventeenth Earl of Nonsuch, the Parachute Regiment. Philip James Nettleship, the Army Dental Corps."'

And now both cricketers and spectators had realized that something peculiar was happening. A crowd began to gather round the two girls and the old man who was kneeling. An officious man came forward.

'I am a *doctor* – ' he began.

'Leave him alone,' said Tessa.

Such was her tone that the man slunk back, while the crowd gabbled, some in his favour, some in Tessa's.

'"Hilary James Royce, the Royal Fusiliers. Percival Nicholas de Courcy Sangster, the Rajputana Rifles. Lancelot Sassoon-Warburton, the Ninth Lancers. Cyprian

Jordan Clement Willard Wyndham Trefusis, Tenth and last Baron Trefoil of Truro, the Sixtieth Rifles. The Honourable Andrew Usquebaugh, Midshipman, the Royal Navy."'

The voice, which had begun to falter, now gained in strength.

'"Richard Valence, the Royal Scots Greys. Andrew Pergamon Vallis, the Coldstream Guards. Allan George Williams, the Sixth Gurkhas. Derek Williams, the Royal Horse Artillery. Geoffrey Alaric Williams, the King's Shropshire Light Infantry. Jonah Zaccarias, the Royal Air Force. Emanuel Zyn, the Pioneer Corps." These, and so many more, that old and feeble and unworthy, I have now forgotten. The chivalry of England, all perished to save their country for touts and rabble.'

An angry chattering came from the group around, as they gathered the old man's drift. The young fiercely repudiated such undemocratic attitudes; the old, whose attitudes these had once been, were reminded that they had been too feeble to sustain them, that they had lost their stomachs for the fight and been unmanned by egalitarian aggression and sanctimonious drivel; the middle-aged, who were approaching the peaks of prosperity and success, were anxious that no utterance be made that might cause question or disruption. All were against the Senior Usher, except for the two girls, whom chance had made his champions as he knelt on the steps and told his litany of vanished honour. By being the first to come upon him and so having heard his dirge from the beginning, they had, in a manner, eaten his salt, and they could never leave him now.

'Touts and rabble,' the Senior Usher repeated in a high clear voice, and fell forward on to the steps above him and into the dark.

PART TWO
The Bower of Bliss

The while some one did chaunt this lovely lay:
Ah! see, whoso fayre thing doest fain to see,
In springing flowre the image of thy day.
Ah! see the Virgin Rose, how sweetly shee
Dost first peep forth with bashful modestee,
That fairer seemes the lesse ye see her may.
Lo! see soone after how more bold and free
Her bared bosome she doth broad display;
Lo! see soone after how she fades and falls away.

So passeth, in the passing of a day,
Of mortall life the leafe, the bud, the flowre;
Ne more doth florish after first decay,
That earst was sought to deck both bed and bowre
Of many a lady, and many a Paramowre.
Gather therefore the Rose whilest yet is prime,
For soone comes age that will her pride deflowre;
Gather the Rose of love whilest yet is time,
Whilest loving thou mayst loved be with equall crime.

Edmund Spenser, *The Faerie Queene*, Book II, Canto
xii, stanzas 74 and 75

'I saw that little partner of yours yesterday,' said Richard Harbinger to Carmilla Salinger in her bedroom and her bed in Lancaster College, Cambridge; 'at that School of his.'

'I thought we weren't talking about him.'

'Oh, I've stopped being jealous in that quarter. I'm only sorry that I was so stupid the other day.'

He raised a stout, stubby, hairy leg perpendicular above them both, then slowly lowered it.

'You see,' said Harbinger, 'I've seen something since then. I've seen young Marius Stern – down at his School.'

'So you have just remarked.'

'I was there to give a lecture. He came to it.'

'He would. He knows a good thing when it's going.'

'He seemed to enjoy it. He asked me a very pertinent question at the end.'

'What did he ask?'

Harbinger paddled four fingers on Carmilla's breasts. Carmilla wished he would go off exploring again. He was quite fun, but only in short bursts. (Perhaps he had reason to be jealous after all.)

'He asked,' Harbinger was saying, 'about the areas that still remained to be explored. Where could I go next, he wanted to know, and actually *explore* as opposed to merely traversing and confirming?'

'And where could you go next?' said Carmilla, trying to keep the eagerness out of her voice.

'The Planets, I told him. But they were too expensive

just now. Under the Ocean – expensive too, but just feasible.'

'Oh,' said Carmilla, briefly envisaging Harbinger as Captain Nautilus saluting in farewell (thank God) from the conning tower of a 1914 submarine. 'When shall you start?'

'Not till I've finished my book. You needn't worry, darling. I shall be around for months yet.' (CHRIST.) 'But what I'm really getting on to is this. After my lecture, Marius came up to me on the dais, to pay the courtesy due to someone with whom he had acquaintance, however slight, and who was now visiting his terrain as a guest. I was wrong about his manners, you see. They are exquisite.'

'Have a care,' said Carmilla; 'it would be unwise in you to fall for Marius.'

'I shall do nothing of the kind, I assure you. When he came up, the master in charge of the lecture, a man called Raisley Conyngham – '

' – Aha,' said Carmilla, 'the Demon King – '

' – He seemed civil enough just then. Later, I began to wonder. Anyway, this Raisley Conyngham said that Marius would be given the afternoon off to take me round the School, if I would like that. Which I would. So off we went, Marius and I, to some of the new Social and Medical Centres – bloody silly, those boys will grow up as soft as turds – and also the New Laboratories and the new Music School and the New Christ knows what. So at last I asked, could we go to see the Chapel, the Memorial Chapel, which I had heard was an interesting example of early thirties ecclesiastical.

'"I'm afraid not, sir," Marius said. "There's a funeral on. The funeral of the last of the Senior Ushers. The whole School is there."

'"Oughtn't you to be?" I said.

'"You heard what Mr Conyngham said, sir. He excused me."

'Well,' said Harbinger to Carmilla, 'I wasn't quite happy about that. There was something, I felt, something not quite right about it.'

'Trust you to poke your nose in,' mumbled Carmilla, who was being half choked with a mouthful of scrotum.

'What was that?'

'Nothing, Dick. Just remarking on your compulsion to explore . . .'

'So I followed the thing up. "Surely Mr Conyngham is not your Housemaster?" I said. "No," Marius said: "he teaches me Greek and Latin Verse." "And does that entitle him to excuse you from Chapel?" "Someone had to take care of you, sir." "I could have done very well on my own – I, of all people – and would of course not have minded being left by myself in these particular circumstances."

'Then there was quite a long silence, while we walked through the Headmaster's Garden – open to all these days, apparently. At length Marius said, "You know the old tale about the ship-wrecked mariner who puts a message in a bottle and commits it to the gods of the Ocean?"

'"Yes," I said. "What's that got to do with your not attending Chapel?"

'"I've decided," he said, "to put a message into a bottle, and let the gods of the Ocean manage its destination and so, quite possibly, mine. Now sir, if I had a bottle with me, the message I should write and put into it would be this: 'I loved the Senior Usher – his marvellous Art Lectures, his soft, worldly remarks, his decency, his fairness, his kindness, his style, his wit. I wished to attend

87

his funeral . . . with my friends who felt likewise. I was prevented, by another man whom I also love, but in a different way. I do not understand the other man's motive; perhaps he is jealous of the dead man's influence, perhaps he thought that if I attended his funeral that influence would be augmented and perhaps more seriously established than before, because of the solemnity and the melancholy of the occasion. But whatever he thought he has acted most cruelly."

'"Then why did you obey him?" I asked. "No man can command you to stay away from a funeral. What would you write, in your message in the bottle, about *that*?"

'"I should write, sir, that I *cannot* disobey him. I might have done once, but no longer. I cannot disobey him without tearing away a part of my entrails."

'And then, Carmilla, darling Carmilla, a very funny look came into his face. A sort of adoration, but not just that. There was also a . . . a look of Cortes about the lad . . . and a look of Faust. For there was not only love here, but also wonderment, at what had been and would be discovered. And one element more: there was unease, suspicion – there was guilt. Whether this outweighed the adoration and the wonderment, I don't know and I don't think the boy himself knew. Probably not; probably the measure was wavering, was slowly sinking the devil's way, and had been, I think, for some time. But there was still something, something quite substantial, in the other scale. There was still, therefore, doubt . . . doubt, which he has decided to cast on the waters in his bottle, that the gods of the Ocean may bring the message to whom they will.'

* * *

Carmilla crossed the Cam by Lancaster Bridge and walked down the Avenue. Nobody, since the removal of the decaying elms, had been able to decide with what to replace them or how to pay for it; and so now the Avenue had become a naked causeway between the lower-lying meadows to left and right.

Carmilla wished to speak to the Provost's secretary, Len, who, it had been deposed to her by one of the servants in the Provost's Lodging, had set off down the Avenue with the Provost himself, not twenty minutes before, on a visit to the Fellows' Garden on the other side of the Queens Road. Since the Provost had a horror of the denuded Avenue, conceiving that he himself had murdered the trees and the tree nymphs by allowing them to be destroyed, it was surprising, thought Carmilla, that he had let himself be taken that way for his walk. Len must have coaxed and bullied: 'Come along, Provost dear,' Len would have said, 'let's have no more nonsense about murdering those elms. They were diseased, and they had to go, and that's all about it.'

A surprising number of people were milling about in the Fellows' Garden: not only the Provost and Len, but Nicos Pandouros and Greco Barraclough with them, to say nothing of Piero Caspar who was walking (prancing) backwards, lecturing the whole group about something as they advanced. Since the Provost walked on a stick, the rate of the march was very slow, and every time Piero and his club foot cavorted away from his audience by as little as three or four steps he had to return by at least two. Also present were Sir Jacquiz Helmutt and his wife, Marigold, with the Helmutt twins, a boy and a girl, fine free-limbed children, perfectly made and proportioned, impassive of face and apparently voiceless, twelve years old to judge by their features, fifteen to judge by the size and the cut of them, though in fact (as Carmilla had been frequently informed) they were not yet ten. Fussing about Sir Jacquiz was his old friend, Ivor Winstanley, the dilatory Latinist (his edition of Cicero's Works in Verse was said to be more than a decade overdue), and mooning about Marigold was Balbo Blakeney, the delinquent biochemist and College Wine Steward.

To none of these people except Len (and perhaps Provost Llewyllyn if he were well enough) did Carmilla wish to speak. She therefore settled herself in a canvas chair in the summer house to wait until the *passaggio* should subside, and took out a paperback edition of Donne's poems as defence against importunity. But she did not read; she thought.

She thought, first, of the Editor of the volume in her hand, who had recently edited and introduced a selection of Latin Verse of the Renaissance which included a more than usually hideous poem about the pox. This she had read in the interest of research: there was something very indicative about the date of the poem – the author of which had died in 1456. Now, she reasoned, if the Great American (Caribbean) pox came back to Europe with Columbus in the late 1490s, the poem in question, having been written in 1456 at the latest, must refer to a pox from some other source, e.g. from the Levant. It was germane to her thesis to prove the existence of such a pre-Caribbean pox, and this was proving unexpectedly diffi-cult, for almost no historian, no scribe, nobody between Thucydides and Defoe had attempted descriptions of diseases and their symptoms detailed and accurate enough to invite diagnosis. In Propertius' Elegies swish and promiscuous tarts went into a sort of consumptive decline, while on the showing of Catullus and occasionally of Horace they just seemed to deteriorate piecemeal through excessive activity and ill-judged choice: but nowhere was a proper clinical survey. (And how should there be in the work of lyricists? Though someone like Pliny might have taken on the task.) The best evidence for a pre-1490s brand of the pox was to be found in lepers' cemeteries, where the remains often showed distinct signs of having been infected by tertiary or quaternary symptoms of the old Raw-Boned Knight, and not by leprosy. But such evidence was difficult and expensive to find, volatile and fissiparous when found. She could, of course, make some use of her immense wealth to obtain and preserve it, but this would be cheating. In the making of her dissertation she must do and make do (she often told herself) as other scholars did.

Next, she wondered what reason had brought so many people into the Fellows' Garden in the morning of the day, a time at which they ought all to be at work; and she concluded that they had been unable to resist the glamour and enticement of the gaudy spring.

Last, and least, she thought of Richard Harbinger, who had left for London (Hail, Mary) and would not be back for four or five days. The trouble was, she reflected, that these days one was not forbidden to harbour one's lovers in the College overnight; unofficially, indeed, this was almost encouraged, even by such reactionary (in other respects) elders as Sir Tom Llewyllyn, the Provost. Mean and predatory paramours took advantage of this. Dick Harbinger could perfectly well afford to stay the night – many nights – in the Blue Boar or the Garden House; instead, he hung around after the performance was over, talking incessantly about himself, his achievements and his intentions. Oh for the old regulations, she thought: all non-members of the College to be *out* by midnight. But then she reflected that, in the days when such regulations

91

obtained, she, as a woman, would never have been allowed *in* – not, that was to say, as an undergraduate, let alone as a Fellow. One must take the rough with the smooth, she supposed; but very soon now she would have had enough of Richard Harbinger, who was really getting very rough indeed, literally and sexually as well as metaphorically. The man had a particularly abrasive beard; he didn't give a damn about whether *she* came or not, he just concentrated on what he wanted her to do to *him*, and positively lectured, indeed harangued, her the entire time she was doing it . . . making sure, as often as not, that she couldn't answer back. Take last night: all that about Marius, on and on and bleeding on.

However, in this one instance she was rather glad he had spoken, even if he had chosen the wrong place and time, because what he had said must now be very rapidly passed on, in several quarters. While Dick might be as annoying and insistent as oestrus and the Dog Star in the role of companion and lover, he was infallibly perspicacious in minding other people's business. In this case, Marius's business. And whereas Marius's affairs had nothing to do with Dick Harbinger and not all that much to do with herself, they had plenty to do with her sister (who was carrying his child), her Provost (who was the boy's uncle by marriage), and many of her acquaintance. '*Res Unius, Res Omnium*,' she now said to herself, quoting the motto of the regiment to which her brother-in-law and many of his old friends (now her new ones) belonged: the affair of one is the affair of all – at any rate when it came to need or peril.

Time to get going, then. The Helmutt party was drifting away down the lawn, sucking Ivor and Balbo along with it. The Provost was still being flirtily entertained by Piero, while Nicos and Greco listened in. Len had turned away from them, and was suspiciously examining the Judas tree, peering round and between its boughs at the departing Helmutts.

Carmilla came up behind him and tweaked the nape of his neck.

'Hello, Lenikins,' she said.

'Darling Carmilla. Pregnant with news. I can tell by the way your eyeballs are swelling. Like balloons, darling.'

'Come into the summer house.'

'You know,' he said as he followed her, 'something will have to be done about those Helmutt twins. They're not right, Carmilla. They've hardly uttered two sentences between them since they were born. They greet or recognize no one, not even their parents.'

'They are obedient,' Carmilla said.

'Yes. It makes it easier to get what they want from Jacquiz and Marigold. They may not converse with them but they do ask for things from time to time.'

'Ask for what?'

'To be taken to certain places. In Europe. Turkey. Egypt. Israel.'

'Do they react to those places?'

'Jacquiz doesn't know. They just look at them through those beautiful eyes of theirs and say nothing, until in due course they ask, very politely, to be taken home again.'

'Balbo Blakeney says they'll just vanish one day. Quite soon, he says. But why should Balbo know?'

'He might. He just might.'

'How?'

'That, my darling Carmilla, is a long and complicated story,* for which there is no time now. What is this news of yours?'

---

* Simon Raven, *The Roses of Picardie*, Blond & Briggs, 1979.

'Marius.'

'Christ. Him again. Well, dish it up, dear, all hot and sizzling.'

'Dick saw him at his School. Dick says he's asking for help. Or not so much asking, but testing Fate by making a signal. "A message in a bottle," he called it, the bottle presumably being Dick. If no one answers or attends to it, he will resign himself to what's coming.'

'And what might that be?'

'Being possessed. Body and soul, Richard thinks.'

'By whom?' asked Len, pretty well knowing the answer.

'A master at his School. Raisley Conyngham. More than just a master at the School. A rich man, the owner of an estate in Somerset and a string of racehorses. A friend . . . or at least an established connection . . . of Giles Glastonbury and that lot.'

'One of whom died in this College not many weeks ago.'

'Yes,' said Carmilla. 'A young cousin, or son of a cousin, whatever that makes him. Myles. The one that used to play Royal Tennis with Theodosia.'

'And the one that fancied *you* . . . If I remember the reports of his death correctly, he claimed that this Raisley Conyngham was somehow responsible for his affliction. Conyngham had touched him, touched him on the hair . . . so he told Fielding Gray just before he died.'

'Which has to be rubbish. Since when did a laying on of hands confer death? But all that is by the way. Our problem, Len – '

' – *Your* problem, darling – '

' – is simply, what should I do now? The message in the bottle has come to shore, you might say, as Marius must have known it would. What does one do about it?'

'One goes to that School of his,' said Len,' and shakes

94

some sense into him. If he knows he is about to be possessed – or is even already possessed – by Raisley Conyngham, and if he dislikes the notion enough to make signals about it, then he can surely fight free of Conyngham's influence.'

'I don't think so. The point was, Dick said, that he probably sent his message *only because* Conyngham had recently upset him, had been unkind to him. He'd prevented his attending the funeral of some old man – the Senior Usher he was called – whom Marius had been fond of. So Marius was in the mood to make a protest, and because Dick was ready to hand he said his piece to him. But when this Senior Usher has been in the earth for a few weeks, and when Conyngham has smoothed Marius down and dispensed a copious dose of . . . of whatever kind of influence he has over him, he'll soon slide back into the old groove. He may have said to Dick, "Please send someone to the rescue", but if, when the rescue party arrives, he is no longer in the mood to be saved, a pretty fair old farce will ensue.'

'So,' said Len, 'you suggest instant action, instant complaint, perhaps, while Marius is still in a pet with Conyngham?'

'Not possible – neither action nor complaint – unless there is proof that something *wrong* is actually in train. Which there isn't. Mere influence is nothing. Schoolmasters are *meant* to exercise influence over their pupils.'

'For good.'

'How prove this is for bad?'

'Wasn't there some very peculiar incident,' said Len, 'last April, on Bellhampton Racecourse? Some account of it dribbled through to me. Marius was acting as groom to one of Conyngham's horses, and there was some kind of stampede? Some wretched child was killed.'

'Marius's friend, Palairet. Theodosia was there and told me all about it later.'

'What do you make of all that?'

'What can we make of it? Horses *do* act up dangerously from time to time, and people *do* get killed by them. No blame attached to anyone. In fact a lot of people behaved rather well, including Raisley Conyngham.'

'Look,' said Len. 'A little while ago Marius was down here – '

' – I saw him – '

' – and came to the Provost's Lodging, by invitation. But the Provost was too ill to see him. While Marius was there, Piero came in and said that what the Provost needed was entertaining company to see him through the summer. Marius said, off the top of his head, without being consulted, without even, really, being spoken to at all, that the chap we needed to amuse the Provost was a friend of his, a school friend called Milo Hedley.'

'Milo Hedley is Conyngham's lieutenant, or familiar. His partner in influencing Marius. I heard a lot about him from Theodosia, who had heard about him from Palairet. Milo Hedley was staying with Conyngham in the Somerset house last Easter, at the same time as Marius was there learning to be a groom.'

'Then Milo Hedley might provide the kind of evidence we need? To mount a rescue operation for Marius?'

'Might,' said Carmilla rather hopelessly. 'Remember he is Conyngham's apprentice – a very apt one.'

'Nevertheless,' said Len, 'I think that I might follow up Marius's suggestion and invite this Milo as company for the Provost . . . and see what he has to say for himself.'

'He won't be able to come till the end of the Quarter at his School. Ages away. Is nothing to be done meanwhile?'

'Yes,' said Len. 'Go to your sister Canteloupe. I have a

hunch that Theodosia, after all that has passed, will be very concerned to hear about Marius. Theodosia, of all people, could have constructive suggestions.'

'Len is a very long time with Carmilla,' grumbled the Provost, Sir Thomas Llewyllyn. He was now sitting on a seat under a cherry tree, bouncing his bottom with irritation. 'What are they talking about?'

'Those Helmutt children,' said Nicos, who had caught a few words as Len and Carmilla had receded into the summer house.

'The sooner *they* take off, the better,' said Piero.

'They are very beautiful,' said the Provost, while Greco Barraclough nodded thoughtfully.

'What makes you think they will take off?' said Greco to Piero.

'Just a little Sicilian hunch, dear,' Piero said. 'They're poised, if you ask me.'

'But they're not ten years old.'

'That won't stop 'em,' said Piero. 'I must go and do some work. The Tripos is upon me.'

Len sauntered over, without Carmilla.

'Where's Carmilla?' said the Provost.

'Gone to make a telephone call.'

'Who to?' persisted the peevish Provost. 'Why is every-one so restless today? Piero worrying about his exams, though he's beastly rich and I'll make him a Fellow anyway. People saying odd things about those delicious Helmutt children and how they're going to run away. And

97

now Carmilla, leaving this lovely garden to make a telephone call.'

'"The world is too much with us," Provost,' said Greco Barraclough.

'That's about it, darling,' said Len. 'Or you could say that spring upsets people. April is the cruellest month, and all that crap.'

Piero, who had observed Carmilla's departure, caught her up on the naked Avenue.

'More bother with Marius Stern?' said Piero.

'How did you know?'

'You had the "Marius" look about you in the garden, a sort of bloated-with-excitement look that everyone gets when Marius is under discussion.'

'I thought you hardly knew him.'

'That is true. But I know a lot of other people who *do* know him. And always, when there is news of Marius Stern, they get that special bulging-eyed "Marius" look.'

'None of which is really your affair,' said Carmilla sharply.

'No? I am a friend of the Provost: Marius is the Provost's nephew by marriage. I notice, incidentally, that you did not bring your news of Marius to *him*.'

'Mind your business, Piero.'

'I was a friend – a very close friend – of the late Ptolemaeos Tunne, who indeed left me a great deal of his money. Ptoly Tunne's niece, Jo-Jo Guiscard (née Pelham) is having a prolonged walk out, under the Pyrenees, with Marius's mother. Or again, I have been intimate with

Baby Canteloupe (née Llewyllyn) your sister's predecessor as Marchioness, Sir Tom's daughter, and Marius's loving cousin. With all this, revered Carmilla, you should understand that Marius may soon become very much my business.'

'Don't meddle, Piero. Don't meddle, or I shall wish you back in your convent in the Laguna Morta. Questions could be asked, you know, about your . . . emergence from there and your actual identity . . . as opposed to the identity which Ptolemaeos Tunne purchased for you.'

'You know nothing about all that,' said Piero, barely managing not to snarl.

'No. But Fielding Gray and his friend – and mine – Jeremy Morrison, know a lot about all that.'

'You are a decent and civilized woman. You would never – '

' – Don't try me, Piero. And just don't meddle. Enjoy Tunne's money. Get a First, become a Fellow of this College, and then a fashionable pundit – all with my blessing. But leave yourself out of *this*, out of all this about Marius. You did enough damage with Jeremy Morrison and Baby. Don't meddle in Marius.'

'My father was an Officer Cadet here,' said Jeremy Morrison, looking out from the balcony of his room over what had once been the British Military Cantonment of Bangalore. 'One of the few places in India with a grass wicket, he used to say. Wasted on him, of course. He always was a wretched player.'

'Not so bad,' said Fielding Gray: 'he played once or

twice for the XI at School in 'forty-five. It was a good XI too.'

'He said there used to be a funfair next to the cricket ground here, to amuse the troops. Can you see a fair ground, Fielding? After all, this is still a garrison town.'

'I dare say that Indian troops are not amused by the English idea of a funfair.'

'Nor were the British troops in my father's day. The funfair was meant to keep them from the women of the houses. But of course there is no substitute for sex.'

'No,' said Fielding. 'Who was that bit of Indian rubbish you dragged back here last night?'

'That "bit of Indian rubbish" was a Naik in the Mysore Lancers. He chose his regiment aptly.'

'I see. First that boy, Milo Hedley. Now, pick-ups in the bazaar. You're getting quite a taste for being laid, aren't you? You'd better watch it, Jeremy. There's a rumour going round of a new and very nasty disease. Carefully designed by God, I hear, for those who offend Him by getting their pleasure – active or passive – *per anum*.'

'What was it that Irishman said? "'Twas God that made this love, not I."'

'Yes. Made it – and cursed it. It's a trick God has, you see . . . offering people prettily wrapped choccies with nasty centres. This is the most unwholesome of any yet.'

'If the rumours are true.'

'There are some people dead of it already. This thing kills, Jeremy, and has no cure. And in any case, you can't tell me that chambering with other ranks of the Mysore Lancers is a good advertisement for your mission. Oneness with the Soil; Absorption in the Universal Mother-hood of the Good Earth – people do not expect the High Priest of such a religion to be a common pathic.'

'The message still seems to be going down well. Remember my reception at Delhi. Mother Teresa wasn't in it.'

'Quite clearly, there are many that think of this as a fertility cult, many that imagine you may have some new secret by which you can increase the yield of their miserable land. Ample cause for mild hysteria – especially as you do not disabuse them of the dream.'

'Nor do I lie to them. I tell them the message, and let them interpret it as they will.'

'What do you want, Jeremy? To get rich quick before you're rumbled?'

'I have a great deal of money already, now that my father has let it flow.'

'Well, then. Do you want to achieve notoriety through deception? To make people hope that there may be, if not a new abundance in their crops, at least a new balsam for their despairing souls?'

'Certainly I do.'

'Knowing that very soon you must be discredited . . . that you will be revealed as a fraud, and that when that happens all the hope you have raised, all the balsam you have spread, will turn to a scorching poison?'

'Why, Fielding, *why* should I be revealed as a fraud?'

'Because you don't believe in any of this. You never did. You just set out to show them all at Lancaster that you too could reach eminence – and much quicker than they ever could, much quicker than poor old Tom Llewyllyn with his history books or pompous Jacquiz Helmutt with his artefacts and excavations. So you preached your gospel plausibly, with much publicity, and without believing a word of it; and when people do that, while they may succeed briefly, they are very soon caught out, usually because they become careless, arrogant or stale. What shall you do when that happens to you?'

'Do stop lecturing, Fielding. You're being a bore.'

'I know. I'll stop – if you'll answer my last question.'

'Right. When and if I'm caught out, since I shall have committed no crime, embezzled no money, taken no life, I shall simply go quietly home and spend the rest of my life fishing with flies for salmon and reading Plato and Virgil (as the saying is) with my feet on the fender. For public life has given me a great yearning for the pleasures of the country, of scholarship and of solitude. Meanwhile, Fielding, the whole point of this circus – have you not guessed, for Christ's sake? – is simply to see just how long I can keep it going, *how long I can take the booby world in*. I am engaged in an experiment – to exemplify and illustrate the credulity of the human race and the sheer farce of human existence. I've already had a very amusing run, and I'm not yet entirely bored with it – despite my longing for the good life of the Sabine farm. So it could have quite a way to go yet. Do you still want to accompany me? Australia next lap: Perth, Adelaide, Melbourne and Sydney – the golden apples, you might say, of the Antipodes.'

Telephoning from Lancaster College to Wiltshire, Carmilla told her sister, Theodosia, levelly and accurately, what Richard Harbinger had said about Marius.

'No proof,' said Theodosia.

'None,' agreed Carmilla.

'You need a concrete instance to show that Conyngham's influence is evil, corrupting or criminal. Now, that business at Bellhampton – it showed nothing of the kind. Not as it appeared to the naked eye. Does Richard think that anything is impending?'

'Perhaps. But he certainly doesn't know what.'

'Tessa,' said Theodosia. 'Tessa Malcolm was staying there with Conyngham in Somerset at the same time as Marius. She was present at the races at Bellhampton – dressed up in some extraordinary way. She may know if there was anything – corrupt or peculiar – behind that mêlée at the meeting. She may know . . . of a pattern or purpose behind it all. She may even know if anything at all definite is planned by Conyngham for the future.'

'Shall you take her on? Or shall I?'

'It had better be me,' said Theodosia. 'I have an entrée.'

'But do you feel up to it?'

'I feel a bit queasy in the mornings. Otherwise okay.'

'And what is this entrée?' Carmilla asked.

'Canteloupe gets an occasional newsletter from his old School. It seems that Tessa Malcolm is a star of the Girls' Under Sixteen Cricket XI. They have a match, very soon, at Hurlingham. Nothing more natural than that I, the sporting girl, should be hanging about at Hurlingham. I should be able to engineer a quiet word with Tessa.'

'Do you know her well enough?'

'We shall be two sporting girls together,' Theodosia said.

* * *

Tessa Malcolm was sick as mud. She had allowed herself to be yorked by a half-volley – only her third ball, after cutting the first two deliciously late for four. Her chum Jakki (twelfth man, as she insisted on calling herself, and scorer) had then annoyed her bitterly by pointing out that this was the third time she had been out that way in the last fortnight. Leaving Jakki a prisoner in the scorers' box, Tessa stomped off round the boundary of the Hurlingham Cricket Ground and soon came to a pretty little copse out of which somebody had shaped a pretty little arbour inside which a long, large yet lissom lady of some twenty-three summers, and dressed in dark grey flannel trousers and a silk cricket shirt, was sitting on a seat.

'Sit you down with me, Teresa Malcolm,' said the lady. 'I'm Theodosia Canteloupe, "Thea" to my friends.'

'Yes, my lady,' said Tessa, 'I remember you very well.'

'"Thea" to my friends, girl. Why do they trick you out in those silly little white skirts? What's wrong with trousers? Not but what you look lovely, but that's not the point.'

'What *is* the point, Thea?' said Tessa. Christ, she thought, is this what it's like? She had seen Thea quite often before, of course, but this was the first time she had ever really seen her. So is this what it's like, she thought, is this what they're all on about, from Sappho to that song about the Isle of Capri? Milo, Rosie, Marius – none of them had made her melt, melt and yet tingle all over with sheer adoration, like this.

'Cricketers ought to wear trousers,' said Theodosia; 'that's the point.'

'I think you're lovely too,' said Tessa, ignoring the polemics.

'So we both know where we are, don't we?' said

Theodosia. Christ, she thought, is it possible to yearn for somebody, like this?

She kissed Tessa on the lips. A shudder ran down from Tessa's hips, over her knees, and rippled among the ginger down just below them.

Tessa raised her face for another kiss.

'Later,' said Thea. 'We shall have time enough for that.'

'All our lives,' said Tessa.

'We must begin,' said Thea, 'by talking of Raisley Conyngham. You spent last holidays at his house in Somerset?'

'Ullacote.'

'With Marius Stern?'

Tessa nodded and held Theodosia's hand.

'Tell me,' said Thea.

'I escaped. They still have Marius.'

They: Conyngham and his henchman, Milo Hedley, Thea thought.

'What will they do with him?'

'They will try to make him do things . . . not so much because they desire them done, though sometimes they may, but for the pleasure of watching him act according to their absolute will and knowing he can do none other.'

'As at Bellhampton?'

'Yes,' said Tessa. 'Only there he was made to *submit* according to their will. But even this submission required very accurate obedience on his part: such an obedience as they could never have obtained from him, without full possession of him. Possession of his spirit.'

'It has come to that?'

'Yes. But I know nothing of their future plans, as I no longer exist for them. Do you know anything . . . darling Thea?'

'Yes, I do. Oh, sweet Tessa. But very little. At Marius's suggestion (why did he make it?) Milo may go to stay in the Provost's Lodging in Lancaster. With Marius's uncle by marriage, Provost Llewyllyn. Why, one wonders again? But whatever the reason, he would not be free to do this until the end of your Quarter.'

'Yes, he would be, Theodosia. We have a break in the middle of the Quarter. Nearly ten days. Mid-June.'

'You will come to me in Wiltshire then?'

'If you please, my lady, if you please. And is that all you know?'

'One more thing. Marius has breached their influence. Enough to cry out to be saved. Though how long he will be sincere in this we do not know.'

'It happens in brief spurts. Last spring at Ullacote, Milo, who did not desire Marius, nevertheless desired to see him dressed as me – and me as Marius.'

'What sort of quirk was that?'

'It had to do with power. Milo wished to convince himself that he was so far in command of Marius and me that he could absolutely dictate our roles even to the extent of making us exchange personalities. I, who at that time worshipped Milo, was willing. Marius rebelled. He would wear my clothes, he said, if Milo wished. But he would not put on a brassière fitted with false breasts, an item as to which Milo was very specific. When Milo still insisted, Marius made to strike him. He flattened his palm and proffered the heel of his hand, ready to aim the blow he had used on poor Pally Palairet at Oudenarde House – straight at the throat. This was enough. Milo just shrugged and went away.'

'So Marius was mutinous,' said Thea. 'On that occasion he protested. And now he seeks salvation.'

'Same thing,' said Tessa. 'To seek escape is the most

radical form of protest. But his resistance did not last long, that time at Ullacote. I do not think it will last long now. Theodosia. Thea. Theodosia.'

'Teresa. Tessa. Teresa.'

'June is near. Birdsong. Do you hear it, Thea? "Against our wedding day, which is not long; sweet Thames, run softly till I end my song."'

'Interesting developments, Lenikins.'

'*Darling* Carmilla . . . ?'

Carmilla and Len sat one each side of Provost Llewyllyn, who had suddenly become so apprehensive of what the dispersed dryads of the College elms might do to him that the College Matron had had to be summoned to sedate him.

'But Provost darling,' Len had said, taking one hand of the Provost as the injection began to act, 'the dryads are all dead. They died with the trees.'

'Their ghosts will want vengeance.'

'Dryads are related to the gods,' Carmilla had said, taking the Provost's other hand; 'the gods, once dead, have no ghosts; nor have their relations, the dryads.'

And now, speaking over the recumbent and unconscious Provost, Carmilla said to Len, 'Theodosia has spoken with Tessa Malcolm – with Teresa, as she now calls her. If you wish, you can get that boy Milo here in June, when his School has a long half Quarter break.'

'The good Sir Thomas certainly needs taking out of himself,' said Len, surveying the crumpled heap between them.

'Item,' said Carmilla. 'Tessa . . . Teresa . . . when told by Thea that Marius was showing signs of wishing to escape from Conyngham's influence, said that while such moods of revolt or revulsion did stir in him from time to time, they did not last. The implication was that when Marius did get recalcitrant, Conyngham or Milo Hedley softened him up with some extra-special treat.'

'Which has probably already been done by now?'

'Or very soon will be. Certainly before any kind of rescue can be justified, let alone carried out. Item,' Carmilla said: 'Theodosia says that Teresa says that Conyngham and Hedley are not so much interested in the things they make Marius do as in the process of making him do them and in the spectacle of his performance. They care more for this performance than they desiderate its consequences – though they always know very clearly what these should be.'

'Presumably, if they are horrid enough, they must lend spice to the spectacle of action that precedes them?'

'Presumably,' said Carmilla. 'But for Conyngham at least the emphasis seems to be on the pleasure of making and initiating the spell, of casting it on Marius and watching him move to its urging.'

'Christ,' said Len; 'God does make them. God does really make them.'

'An interesting postscript,' said Carmilla. 'Nothing to do with Marius, but with our old chum Fielding Gray.'

'What's *he* done now? Slept with the Pope?'

'Caused a minor stir with his Memoirs.'

'I didn't think they were finished yet. Let alone published.'

'They're not. But the *Observer* is very keen to publish extracts from the first half of them, and so is the *Perth Envoy* and the *Adelaide Angelus*.'

108

'Oz papers?'

'Yes. A lot of Fielding's family on his mother's side emigrated to Australia.'

'I always thought he had convict blood in him,' said Len: 'something to do with that one eye of his.'

'He wasn't born like that. His face was wrecked by a bomb in Cyprus.'

'No doubt he was putting it where it wasn't wanted,' said Len.

'He was simply doing his duty as an army officer.'

'Yes,' said Len, 'putting his face where it wasn't wanted.'

The Provost began to shift and whimper between them.

'I thought he was meant to be under for a good six hours,' said Len.

'Perhaps it's only a dream?'

'Tullia,' whined Sir Thomas, 'where have they taken you – the ghosts?'

He shifted again and then was still.

'He always blamed those tree nymphs for what happened to his daughter.' Len said. 'Poor Tullia. Poor Baby.'

'Poor Baby – nothing,' said Carmilla, hard as cut glass; 'she made trouble everywhere she went. She couldn't even make Sarum properly. Theodosia's having to do the job all over again. Much against her will.'

'So I have inferred. Tell me, Carmilla: if Theodosia delivers a bouncing boy, Sarum will be superfluous. So . . . what are the plans for Sarum?'

'Sarum isn't my problem.'

'But the enquiry – do admit, darling – is of interest. And could be pertinent to you, no matter what you say. After all, whatever arrangements are made for Sarum, your sister and your brother-in-law are bound to be involved in them.'

'But not I. I have enough to do busying myself with Marius. Strictly, he's not my concern either. But somehow – after what Dick said – it's all been more and more thrust upon me.'

'Well, then. Marius is one of the principal actors in the whole of the affair.'

'Only an understudy.'

'Understudy for Canteloupe himself. The onlie begetter, you might say. The begetter of this new heir and therefore of the problem about the old one. No, darling Carmilla: if you persist in taking on Marius – '

' – Somebody must – '

' – then you take on the problems which his actions promote. For these will rise up against him to accuse his conscience; and of this conscience you have made yourself the keeper.'

Raisley Conyngham steered his rowing boat (the *Palinurus*) into a little creek of the River Wey about halfway between Farncombe and Guildford. Milo Hedley shipped the oars. The bows nuzzled into a bank of reeds and mud. The waters lapped about the midships and the stern.

'When?' said Milo.

'When what, dear boy?'

'When do we brief Marius and oblige Canteloupe? What is the matter with this coming half Quarter? 'Twere best quickly done, Raisley.'

'When you leave this school at the end of the Quarter,

you may call me "Raisley" or "Conyngham" as you will. Until then, you will address me as "sir".

'Then 'twere best quickly done . . . sir.'

'No, Milo. 'Twere best very slowly done. The longer it takes, the longer we may relish the proceedings. And then think what is required: a long sequence of absolutely ordinary events, each following normally from the last, and finally bringing about the desired result so naturally that it provokes the minimum of remark, no guilt, blame nor accusation, no surprise and no shame . . . and at the same time has something dignified and even endearing about it, so that gentle words of pity and commiseration, if not quite of encomium, may be carved on Sarum's stone.'

'I see what you mean, sir. Canteloupe seemed to be thinking of a monument, or at least a sarcophagus.'

'With no ghosts or Furies in the region of either. So we proceed with decorum.'

'Indeed, sir. But at some stage Marius must be briefed.'

'As late as possible. For the sake of discretion.'

'But he *must* be prepared, sir, in good time.'

'Prepared, certainly. Mentally and physically prepared, but with no immediate act assigned or order issued. The sequence of events (which will lead to the quiet and untroubled tomb) can be and must be set in train without Marius's particularly noticing, without his making very much of it. The . . . Prime Mover . . . must be bland and casual. The whole thing must be *distanced*. This will be managed by me, during the break at half Quarter. While you are acting as the Ambassador of the School in the Provost's Lodging at Lancaster (amusing the good Provost and teasing secrets out of his henchman), Marius and I will be following in the footsteps of another distinguished Lancastrian, one Montague Rhodes James. We shall be *antiquarians*, Milo, in the area of Wells-Juxta-Mare and Holkham. There I shall soothe any resentment Marius may still entertain against me for preventing his attendance at the funeral of Nestor (so to speak), indulge him in some small matter which should please him – '

' – What matter, sir?'

' – Give him an agreeable time, Milo, full of the good food and intelligent discourse which he enjoys, and also promise him the passage, for which he hankers, out to his friend Jeremy Morrison this summer. As it happens, Morrison has offered to pay for his ticket, but I can contrive that I should be the one bathed in his gratitude, by my very clemency in granting him permission to go.'

'But he can't go. We shall need him here this summer. Unless, that is, your sequence of normal events is to be stretched so far and so fine that it will snap.'

'Do not worry, Milo. Marius's visit to the missionary Morrison will form part of the sequence.'

'You mean . . . you only have to twitch the thread to bring him back when needed?'

'Something like that,' said Raisley Conyngham. 'But let us return to our little expedition – Marius's and mine – to the Norfolk coast. Dunes, conifers, vast beaches with ridges and quicksands; saltmarshes and ruins (from Saxon chapels to American gun sites); the setting for so many stories of M. R. James. Have you read them, Milo?'

'I have no time for ghost stories, sir.'

'Silly, intolerant boy . . . Somewhere in all of this the sequence will begin – while Marius as yet scarcely remarks its beginning – the sequence of events which will bring Sarum of Old Sarum, without pain or fear or even notice, to his comfortable and honourable grave.'

* * *

On a bandstand in the gardens of Adelaide, not far from the public entrance to the Oval, a Combined British Cavalry Band (on a goodwill visit to Australia) was playing a lively yet somehow haunting air.

'Stop,' said Fielding Gray to Jeremy Morrison. 'Christ, man, it's *Rory Gilpin* . . .'

'What can you mean?'

'*Rory Gilpin*. The March of the tenth Sabre Squadron. The regiment – Hamilton's Horse – had one march, *Prince Harry* it was called, but in the tenth Sabre Squadron we had our own. *Rory Gilpin*.'

'I see, old man,' said Jeremy, and stood still by Fielding.

Fielding's eyes pricked. 'Christ, Jeremy,' he said. '. . . So the cavalry still has its uses. A performance of some versatility,' as he opined later in their Travel Lodge.

'I hope that Serjeant-Trumpeter will perform with equal versatility – *mutatis mutandis*,' Jeremy said.

'For Christ's sake, Jeremy. They're leaving by air at ten P.M for Alice.'

'Just five hours then. Say four, if they have to be at the airport an hour before take-off. Four hours in which to enjoy pneumatic bliss.'

'I'm looking forward to your half Quarter leave,' said Rosie to Tessa, as they walked down Pall Mall towards the National Gallery. 'Let me see. It starts a fortnight from last Friday, and today is Sunday, so there's only twelve days to go. And you'll be at home – for how long?'

'Eight days,' said Tessa: 'but I shan't be at home.'

Rosie carefully said nothing. She did not want to spoil Tessa's Sunday home from School by being inquisitive or possessive, the less so as something in Tessa's voice told her that such Sundays were now to be much fewer. Whatever was claiming Tessa for the half Quarter exeat would probably not stop there. She therefore kept a wary silence as they walked up the steps from Trafalgar Square to the loggia and through the entrance, maintained it as they went past a uniformed official (who dutifully stared at them with piercing and piecemeal lechery, in case they were carrying a bomb), and continued to maintain it until they were in front of the pictures which they had come to see, in the basement. These were four huge pieces by Horace Vernet, whom Tessa had muddled up with his father. So where they were expecting four depictions of the Seasons they found four Napoleonic battles instead.

'I didn't know you weren't coming home for your half Quarter,' Rosie said casually; 'where are you going?'

'These are the wrong pictures,' said Tessa crossly. She consulted a glossy handbook. 'The ones I wanted are in the Musée Calvée in Avignon. By *Claude-Joseph* Vernet.'

'There is one by Claude-Joseph upstairs,' said Rosie, anxious to be helpful. She ran one hand down her black hair, from scalp to shoulder-blade. 'Daddy and I looked at it once. Some eighteenth-century tourists in pretty clothes in a jolly little harbour near Naples. And what Daddy described as "loose washerwomen", only I read somewhere later that they were really collecting shellfish.'

'Let's go and see it, then. I expect it's near the Claude Lorraines.'

'But first,' said Rosie, 'we should look at what is here. At this one.'

The paintings were arranged, on the inner wall of the circular chamber, at the four cardinal points of the

114

compass. The one Rosie had chosen for inspection was at the north of the circle, therefore facing south.

'This is the yard of a large farmhouse or the court of a small manor house,' Rosie said. 'The General – the one in the blue and silver with the tricolor cockade in his hat – is sitting on horseback with some members of his staff. Another important officer in blue and silver is being carried away on a stretcher of muskets and blankets. Here, at the end of the yard, at the bottom centre of the painting.' She pivoted to look at Tessa.

Tessa nodded and smiled.

Rosie pivoted back. 'He has lost his cockaded hat. He is very pale. He is wounded to the death, and he and the stretcher-bearers know it. So does the General at the top end of the yard. He is paying no attention to the arrival of the Galloper. He is watching them carry away his friend. For they *were* friends,' said Rosie; 'see how they are waving to one another. The General is lifting his white-gloved hand, half in farewell and half in benediction, and making little motions of distress with his fingers. The other one has lifted one hand with his palm towards the General, saluting him as the victor and at the same time bidding him goodbye for ever.

'Now let us go and see the *Claude-Joseph* Vernet,' said Rosie, prinking on her thin legs up the spiral stair to the ground floor, 'and also Claude Lorraine's *Enchanted Castle*. What a lot of Claudes for one afternoon.'

'I am sorry I am leaving you,' said Tessa, 'at half Quarter. And for longer than that, I fear.'

'Don't be. I don't suppose you can help it. I shan't pry. I don't really want to know – not topographically, so to speak – where you are going, though I rather think your Auntie Maisie may. See here now,' said Rosie, '*The Enchanted Castle on the Shore*, otherwise known, my

115

Daddy said, as *The Palace of Eros*. Of love. Keats adored this picture, my Daddy said; for see here, Tessa, the "magic casements opening on the foam/Of perilous seas in faery lands forlorn." And so now you are going, I suppose, to the Palace of Eros. You were bound to, fairly soon. And here am I' – she pointed to a dark female figure, crouched in a wilderness beneath the ramparts – 'excluded.'

'You will get in later.'

'Oh yes,' said Rosie. 'It's all entirely natural and *comme il faut*. You are the older: my turn next. I'm not complaining.'

No, thought Tessa, she really isn't: she knows that when one is called to the Enchanted Castle one must go there; but all the same I have hurt – hurt so cruelly – her sad little sense of honour.

'The thing is, Provost,' said Milo Hedley, 'that the more perceptive of the young are beginning to find "the permissive society" exceedingly dull.'

Milo was walking with Len and the Provost in the Provost's enclosed garden, outside the windows of his withdrawing room. It had been arranged that he should come to the Lodging in Lancaster for some days of the half Quarter exeat, on the pretext of 'liaising' between the School and the University, though the real reason was to see whether he would be up to 'amusing' the Provost for a longer period later in the summer, after the School holidays began. As things stood now, Milo was making a very good fist of amusing the Provost and an even better one of alienating everyone else, with the possible exception of Len. Piero Caspar and Nicos Pandouros came to the Lodging as little as possible after their first meeting with Milo, and Carmilla Salinger came not at all. Epithets applied by them to Milo were variously 'oily', 'conceited', 'creepy', 'slimy', 'saurian', or, *tout court*, 'snake'. Milo, said Piero, was 'snake' – not *a* snake but just 'snake', which was to say the Platonic idea of snake-substance as laid up in the Ideal Realm. The truth was, of course, that Milo had made Piero, Nicos and Carmilla exceedingly jealous by his *succès fou* with the Provost.

'In the permissive society,' Milo was saying now, 'sexual pleasure has none of the heady fascination induced by moral guilt, none of the *frisson* lent by fear of being caught and punished. Venereal disease is readily preventable and, if contracted, readily curable. Sex, Provost, has become a bore, or at best a hygienic exercise for ridding oneself of superfluous fluids.'

He's pitched his level just right, thought Len. Sophisticated, paradoxical, but with a basically simple argument which the Provost can follow quite easily despite the flagging pace of his intellect.

'All of which is all very well, dear boy,' the Provost said, 'but people seem to go on having quite a lot of it.'

'Habit,' said Milo, 'or, as I was saying just now, for the purpose of glandular evacuation. Or simply because they are too unimaginative or too stupid or too wanting in taste to think of any other way of passing the time.'

'Like reading? Or the arts?'

'Certainly. Or like plotting, Provost: intriguing. Emotional or social engineering.'

Now he's gone too far, thought Len: Tom would never approve this kind of exploitation.

Nor did Sir Tom approve: but that did not mean that

he was not interested, as Milo started an elementary account of the theory (in which he had plainly been instructed by a more mature mind) of moral manipulation, of achieving certain ends – good or bad – by the discreet, indeed unnoticed, deployment of certain persons, their talents or their frailties.

'If you encourage a man in the use of an ability or a vice for which he is well known,' said Milo, 'his behaviour will not be noticed. Everyone will just say, "There's X, at it again, translating Herodotus' History or touching up Sea Scouts": entirely predictable behaviour of little intrinsic interest. It follows that if you, so to speak, divert, angle, aim or adjust this behaviour so that it may bring about an end which you desire, you will never be discovered because the means you have employed are everyday phenomena and the end that has resulted from such phenomena will be seen as a necessary consequence of them – as something which, however painful on the one hand or pleasing on the other, had an entirely obvious and natural and unsensational cause; so that deliberate foul play can never be suspected, no blame can ever be imputed, no accusation can ever be preferred.

'For if X falls off a cliff while spying on Sea Scouts who are bathing naked, no one will ever know that it was *you* that directed him, through a long chain of casual and unwitting informants, to the loosest and most treacherous overhang. People will just say: "X up to his old tricks again; no good could ever have come of it." Or again, if one's pupil or protégé wins a brilliant prize for a classical essay, nobody is to know that one has quietly directed his attention (for plausible reasons that ostensibly have nothing to do with the essay prize) to those passages of Herodotus' History by which Y, one of the judges this year, is particularly fascinated. People will just say, if they say anything at all, "How lucky for young Tyro that he shared X's obsession with Xerxes."'

'And you find such skulduggery of interest?' said the Provost mildly.

'The instances I have given, Provost, are very simple. Imagine a whole chain of events, dividing and ramifying, reuniting, returning in on themselves, and then expanding yet again, all stemming (as calculated) from one unnoticed and utterly ordinary word or action. It has the beauty and fascination of a mathematical series. One little remark, Provost; or a suggestion; or an invitation: "Come with me next week to watch the Varsity Match from the Pavilion at Lord's." But the inviter knows that the invited man has been expelled from the MCC for petty pilfering in the changing rooms attached to the Squash Court. Either the invited man must confess to this, or (which is much more likely) he will utter some excuse. If the excuse is genuine, of course, the series stops there. But if it is not, the inviter has an initial hold – slight but real – on the invited. This hold can be used in a number of ways: possibly to embarrass the victim in front of a close friend or relative (why not his mother?), thus making him angry or nervous or resentful or dejected, in any case impairing his powers of judgement and making him more easy to use and control during the next stage of the events in train.'

'What a pity,' chuckled the Provost, 'that you are not coming to this College. We could have had such fun trying out your theories on the more unattractive of the left-wing Fellows.'

Len, feeling it was time that Milo was put in the wrong about something, recalled to him his remarks about the dullness of sex now that guilt and punishment and disease were no more. Conceding that guilt might indeed have ceased to be a factor in sexual behaviour, 'It is still easily

119

possible,' he said, 'to choose some *extreme* form of sex which carries high social penalties. As for disease, there are, as you may have heard, rather alarming rumours from the United States and from Africa.'

'Always something new out of Africa,' interjected Provost Llewyllyn,' and usually something nasty.'

'Tell me more,' said Milo, who had not yet heard, to vulpine Len, who was·wearing a shirt of the Campbell tartan with a tie of the College summer pattern – white with thin stripes of royal purple.

'Nothing much to tell,' said Len: 'not yet. Rumours of an incurable disease which destroys one's powers of resistance even to the most trivial infection and is distributed by sexual – most notably anal – activity.'

'That,' said Milo with relish, 'really *will* get 'em sweating and squealing with terror. A threat to human rutting for the first time in three decades – a whole generation.'

He directed the party to the sundial.

'I adore sundial mottoes,' he said.

'This one,' said the Provost, 'was chosen by Monty James.'

'The writer of ghost stories?' said Milo, remembering Conyngham's reference to these some days before.

'Also a very distinguished scholar. Read his chosen motto to us, Milo.'

'"*Tu pias laetis animas reponis sedibus*,"' read Milo, who had examined the dial the previous day and looked it all up overnight. 'Horace: tenth ode of the first book.'

'Good boy. Now translate.'

'"You", referring to Mercury, "bring the souls of the righteous to the abodes of bliss."'

'Monty James wasn't thinking much of Mercury when

120

he chose this,' said Tom Llewyllyn; 'he was thinking of Time.'

'There are others that take on the office,' said Milo, 'apart from Mercury and Time. It is, I think, an honourable function. For it is often necessary or desirable that souls should be transferred from this world to the next rather more swiftly than would normally be the case. The series of moral or social mathematics about which I have been talking, Provost, often have this end in view.'

'Murder?'

'No. Setting up an entirely natural and normal sequence of events which may lead, without drama or distress, to a decease devoutly to be wished for any number of sound reasons.'

'Oh,' said Tom, looking rather hurt. 'Isn't that rather overdoing it? I feel a little tired, dear boy. Would you bring me to my bedroom, where I shall rest until dinner?'

The thing is now much clearer, thought Len, as the Provost slowly departed on Milo's arm. These theories that that boy is spouting derive from an adult who has influenced him, probably that schoolmaster of whom we have heard talk, Raisley Conyngham. Not content with airing the theories, young Milo is itching to apply them. He loves talking of the matter, so he talks of it to his new friend, the Provost, who does not properly understand what he is saying. He also enjoys danger (welcomes the idea of a new and fiendish sexual disease); so he hints, without committing himself at all plainly, that he is interested in, and may become involved in, the formulation of some series in what he calls human engineering or socio-moral mathematics that may result in somebody's death. He likes throwing out hints because of the small but piquant danger that he may be caught out. The Provost will not catch him out; I might. What does he think I should do if I did? He thinks I should do nothing, because I should be able to do nothing: on his view of the theory – a view no doubt inculcated by Conyngham – these 'series' of events are so cleverly initiated and manipulated to resemble absolutely normal and unremarkable occurrences that, however horrible the result, no one can be accused of contriving it.

This boy Milo, thought Len, is of course the friend of Marius Stern, who introduced him to our notice. Is Marius to be part of Milo's machinations? If so, should I warn Marius's friends? Carmilla? Theodosia? The Provost, for that matter, who is Marius's uncle? No, thought Len. I do not know enough to start being officious. I shall just sit still and watch the thing go on. It promises rich entertainment; the theory is an amusing one, and it will be very enjoyable to see whether it is sustained by its practice.

Marius Stern and Raisley Conyngham were spending their half Quarter exeat at the Regina Hotel (one star, no credit cards accepted) in the hamlet of Holkham.

'A hostelry distinguished by a plain yet savoury cuisine and wonderful surroundings,' Raisley said as they arrived; 'do not make the mistake common among rich young men, my dear Marius, of despising the economic family hotel. Many of them retain the dignity and reticence that has now entirely deserted the great ones, even the Ritz itself.'

For the most part Marius and Raisley drove to cathedrals, churches, castles, abbeys and fine houses; but on two occasions they walked by the sea – or as near as one can get to it at Holkham, where it is seldom much less than a mile away over a treacherous beach. They would leave the Regina, walk down the old road over the level crossing of the coastal railway (long since dismantled) and on towards the dunes and the pine forest that overlook the sands. From here the sea could just be glimpsed, a thin band of turquoise beyond steep ridges and sudden depressions, the latter often of quicksand. One now had a choice between a rough path that led along the line where the dunes meet the beach and another, rather more commodious, path behind the dunes and the ranks of pines, between the forest and an inland saltmarsh. Raisley preferred the path by the beach; he loved, he said, to look at the faraway and so, in this instance, 'never sounding' sea. So this path they took, going south towards Wells, because if one went north the pines became fewer and fewer until they vanished, leaving one on a twisting and ill-marked track between distressful clumps of thorn, thistle, burr and briar.

'Ah, these pines,' Raisley said on their second walk that way; *very M. R. Jamesy*, my dear. You know his stories? The ones set in this part of the world?'

'Only *The Three Crowns of East Anglia*.'

'By no means the best. You must have read *Whistle and I'll Come to Thee, My Lad*?'

'No, sir. I was just going to, once, only my father borrowed my copy to take away with him to Trieste – whence, as you may know, he did not return. We'd had a very funny afternoon – the last afternoon I ever saw him. But I'm sorry, sir, I'm interrupting you . . .'

'Fascinating,' said Raisley. 'Your last afternoon with your father. Go on, Marius.'

'He and my mother came and took me out from my School at Sandwich. We went to see a very creepy

Norman Chapel, hidden away in a large wood, just off the road between Deal and Dover. My mother told me the legend about it – there'd been some Abbess from a nearby Convent who met her lover there. But now it was dank and ruined, unfit for love any more, and absolutely deserted except for a woman, whom my father saw, all alone in a cape. After the Chapel we went to Deal for tea at Mr Brown's Restaurant, and my mother made a row because the anchovy toast, which was famous, had run out when we ordered it. But before we went to Mr Brown's, sir, we went to a lovely secondhand bookshop – '

' – I know it. Just opposite the Royal Hotel – '

' – Super place, the Royal Hotel. Almost built on the beach. But not so famous for teas as Mr Brown's, sir, which is why we went on there from the bookshop – where my mother had seen and bought a copy of M. R. James's *Ghost Stories of an Antiquary*.

'"I'm going to buy you this," my mother said, "as a memento of the afternoon. And of your first ghost."

'"I didn't see a ghost, mummy."

'"Neither did I. But your father did. That woman he told us about – in a cape, near the Chapel."

'"What is this rubbish you talk, Isobel my wife?" my father said. He spoke to her like that sometimes, in a Jewy sort of way, as a joke.

'"No other explanation," my mother said. "Where did she come from, that woman? Where did she go to?"

'"There *was* another car there, Mummy. Under the bank where we parked."

'"Yes. But it belonged to that cross-looking man who came walking down the track, from another part of the wood, and drove away in it – *alone*. So that woman was nothing to do with him."

124

'"Talk about looking cross," my father said, "that woman in the cape would have won a prize. Cross, resentful, miserable . . ."

'"It *must* have been that Abbess," my mother said, "the one that used to have it off in the Chapel with the Lord of the Manor. He went away and left her, so she had plenty to be cross about. Though why *you* saw her," she said to my father, "and Marius and I did not, is an interesting question. And even if it wasn't the Abbess," she said, "this will make a nice present for Marius. They don't do M. R. James in single volumes any more, only in nasty collected editions. So this is something of a rarity – and it includes his best story of all – *Whistle and I'll Come to Thee, My Lad*."'

'But your father borrowed the book, you say, and took it off to Trieste?'

A breeze idled through the pines.

'After tea, sir, on the way back to my School in Sandwich, he asked if he could borrow it. He was in a mood for ghost stories, he said. My mother told him not to be awkward: "I've only just given it to Marius," she said. But when *he* said that the book would remind him, on the journey, both of me and of her, she gave up her objection straightaway. "Silly old Jewboy," she said, and leaned over from the driving seat of her Lagonda and kissed him on the ear. That made me happy, sir. And then I was dropped in the school drive . . . and went off with my friend, Palairet . . . And my father took the book to Trieste. My mother told me later that she made sure to pack it for him. But we never found it after . . . after he was taken from us.'

'He was *not* taken from you,' commented Raisley very firmly; 'he died. He was, in this instance, killed. Never use middle-class euphemisms, Marius. I'm surprised at you.'

'At any rate,' said Marius, 'he went off to Trieste with the book and didn't bring it back.'

'So you've never read *Whistle and I'll Come to Thee, My Lad*?'

'No, sir.'

'The story happens in a place near here,' said Raisley Conyngham. 'Huns'ton or Brancaster, I'd say, because there is a golfcourse. A don on holiday finds an antique whistle, buried near a Roman altar on a path over the golfcourse from the beach to the Dormy House or Hotel. That fits Huns'ton, absolutely. He tries blowing the whistle – and summons Something up.'

'Summons what up?'

'You well may ask, Marius.'

The breeze in the pines grew stronger. Surface sand scurried along the beach. Raisley looked towards the sea. A purple cloud was rising in the east.

'About turn,' said Raisley. 'If we don't loiter we shall have ample time to get back to the Regina before the storm breaks.'

They started back along the path at a steady heavy infantry pace.

'What was the Something which the don summoned up with the Roman whistle, sir?'

'No one ever found out. Not precisely. But it was some kind of . . . energy . . . that turned ordinary draperies – a curtain, for example, or a blanket – into a prowling figure, a prowling and *groping* figure, Marius, so that whatever it was it was obviously blind. And a good job too, because the figure had a face of intense malignance. One night a sheet got off the spare bed in the don's room,' said Raisley Conyngham, 'and started groping after the don.'

Marius giggled.

'Did it find him, sir?'

'The don's golfing partner, a colonel from India, came in just in time, in response to the don's shrieks of terror, and broke it all up. You see, Marius, the energy that transformed the sheet, powerful *in posse*, was improperly directed, undisciplined. It just vanished as soon as the colonel came in with a candle.

'Now,' said Raisley Conyngham as a great portcullis of lighning forked into the sea on his right. 'Now,' said Raisley Conyngham again: 'our problem, yours and mine, is, first, to summon energy, physical, intellectual and moral energy . . . moral in the sense that, though not necessarily righteous itself, it can move in the sphere frequented by righteousness. All these kinds of energy we must summon. Secondly, we have to make sure, Marius, that the vehicles which we employ our energy to propel do not just grope and grovel blindly and collapse as soon as challenged, but continue on their mission or missions unperturbed.'

'We must make sure *our* energy has eyes to command,' Marius said.

A grumbling blast of thunder moved over the beach.

'Good. We must also ensure, of course, that whatever vehicle our energy inhabits and drives does not have a malignant or an evil countenance. Because if it does, someone will grow suspicious or frightened, and challenge it. We do not want it to be challenged even if it is equal to a challenge. We want it to proceed unnoticed on its way.'

'But first we must summon it, sir. Where is our whistle?'

Raisley Conyngham gripped Marius by the shoulder and looked into his eyes. 'I summon it – thus,' he said. A

127

single strip of lightning flickered, and was followed by a growl and a clatter.

'And my vehicle . . . sir?'

'Yourself . . . and such other as you may, from time to time, be instructed to use . . . or any that, on your own responsibility, you see fit to use. Thus, although you knew nothing of what was to come, you suggested that Milo be a guest in the Lodging of the Provost of Lancaster. You did not know it at the time, but you made of Milo Hedley a vehicle.'

'What will he do to help us?'

'He will be tactless, indiscreet and probably boastful; he will cause people to think that *he* is the energy and others (including you) the vehicles which he chooses; whereas *you*, Marius, are the energy, summoned by me; and you and I will choose the vehicles. The misconceptions put about by Milo will confuse and obscure those whom we wish confused and that which we wish obscured.'

'They are not wholly misconceptions, sir. On your showing I *am* one of the vehicles.'

'But driven and navigated only by yourself – not by Milo, as he will imply to others.'

'And whither, sir, am I to navigate?'

'To Canteloupe's house in Wiltshire. Think about it, boy, and all that is in it.'

'I do think about it, sir, and have been for some time. And one of the things that I have thought is that if my lady is brought to bed of a fine boy, then it might be convenient to some that that boy's elder half-brother, as the world will recognize and rank him, should kiss the world goodnight.'

'Would you yourself share some such view?'

'Very probably, sir,' said Marius. 'The older boy is

128

horrible and is apparently becoming daily more so. The younger will be my son, and I would therefore wish him a great inheritance, even though I can never claim him.'

'You are a credit to humanity, Marius, as well as to your tutor.'

As they walked over the old level crossing, the lightning sizzled to earth beyond the pines and the thunder followed it almost instantly.

'One more thing,' said Raisley Conyngham. 'We need a Prime Movement to set the train of events going. Though you are propelling and navigating yourself in your own vehicle, you will need . . . circumstances . . . to which you may respond. You will need something to suggest, or even necessitate, your first motion . . . after which you will readily determine them for yourself.'

'I think that the man with the whistle should arrange the Prime Movement.'

'So do I. Only I am to be saved a difficult exercise in judgement, as the Prime Movement will arrange itself. In August, Marius, my lady Canteloupe will be subjected to one of those clever modern tests which will determine whether she is carrying a boy or a girl. As soon as this is known, both her ladyship and the Marquess Canteloupe are going to adopt certain attitudes. If the child is to be a boy, the attitudes are going to be very simple and definite. If not, there is going to be an element of indecision. But either way, Marius, these attitudes will be enough to set you moving, and to point you in the first direction which is to be taken. Until then, get on with your work and your play . . . of which more presently . . . and forget the whole matter of the House of Sarum.'

* * *

129

Tessa and Theodosia walked in the Rose Garden of Canteloupe's demesne.

'What is that hideous noise, coming from over there?' said Tessa, pointing in the direction of Cant-Fun, where the proles paid their mite to maintain Canteloupe.

Theodosia explained this. Then, 'You're not meant to be able to hear it,' she said. 'This place was designed to exclude all sight and sound of Cant-Fun. And it always has done. *I* can't hear anything.'

'You'd be used to it by now.'

'But I never have heard anything.'

A uniformed nanny approached with a large black pram.

'Sarum,' said Thea. 'Do you want to see him?'

'Yes.'

Peering into the pram, Tessa saw a wrinkled little satyr with thick down on his chin.

'Hullo, Tullius,' she said – for that, she knew, was the satyr's Christian name.

Tullius did not answer.

'He's asleep,' said the nurse.

'His eyes are open.'

'He's still asleep, miss.'

'He's quite well, Daisy?' said Theodosia to the nurse, who was between ginger and auburn in her colouring, and might, only a few years ago, have resembled Tessa.

'Quite well, my lady. Even energetic at times.' Daisy chuckled.

Theodosia did not pursue the topic. 'That is the heir,' she said as the pram rolled away, 'who will be replaced by the child I am carrying.'

'Replaced?' said Tessa. 'But if he is the heir now, he will remain the heir.'

'Exactly so. Abnormal, as you saw, but perfectly well – even, as Daisy said, energetic at times.'

'Then how will it all be arranged?'

'I don't know,' said Thea. 'I simply do what I can to oblige those whom I love. For many years I have loved Canteloupe, in a way: so when he asked me . . . to conceive a child by another man . . . I did so. What is to happen to Tully Sarum must be his decision. He ordered the creation of Tullius, out of his first wife and by an old friend, in the same way as he ordered the creation of the new child out of me.'

'By whom?' said Tessa. 'You will tell me? After the promises we have made?'

'Yes. I shall. By Marius Stern.'

Tessa gave a sudden little skip in her walk.

'He is only fifteen.'

'So are you. He was well up to his task.'

'Then it should be a fine child. I should have been very jealous, once, that Marius should know your body and not mine. That you should know his and not I.'

'I hated his knowing mine. I hated knowing his.'

'You were . . . cold?'

'If only I had been. He stirred me to the verge of frenzy. That is what I hated. That I should be in danger of losing all control of myself.'

'But . . . darling Theodosia. Since I have been here, you have – several times – lost control of yourself. So have I.'

'That is different. It is gentle, it just happens. Without struggle, without effort. It washes over and into me.'

'I know. But still, you lose control of yourself. Something happens which you cannot stop.'

'I don't want to stop it . . . with you. With Marius I did. It would have been violation. So I stopped it, at the last possible moment. He was very surprised and hurt.'

'Now, in any case, you are to bear his child. You will let me bear it with you.'

'Yes. Oh yes.'

'I can come for the School holidays, in August and September? Your husband will not mind?'

'He will be delighted that I have such company. But what about your aunt? She will want you, I think.'

'Perhaps. But she will let me be away, most of the time. She likes to be in London herself, but she thinks the air – and the people – are bad for me.'

'The people?'

'Foreigners. She is very old-fashioned.'

They went through a gate and out of the Rose Garden, then along a stream, which ran across a meadow towards a copse of lady-birch.

'Peace,' said Tessa. 'No more row from Cant-Fun.'

'I cannot understand that,' said Theodosia; 'none of us hears the racket when we are walking in the Rose Garden. It was all very cleverly designed, with specially calculated angles and volumes, by a chum of the Canteloupes – mine and the one before – who was a scientist, a biochemist, also an amateur of architecture.'

'Yet I can hear the row when I'm in that garden. What will they do with that . . . that child, Theodosia? Sarum?'

'I do not know. They will not consult me.'

'Ought we to worry?'

'We ought. But I cannot worry about that thing in the pram.'

'The nurse will protect it, I think. She loves it.'

'Come into this grove,' said Theodosia. 'There is a secret way, the only way. Canteloupe showed me, soon after we were married.'

132

They came to a tiny pool in the centre.

'Here on this grass. Teresa.'

'Theodosia.'

After a time, Tessa said: 'I do not think it much matters how they dispose of Sarum himself, provided they are humane, as why should they not be? But I think others may be injured. That nanny; and whomsoever they use . . . for the act itself.'

'If we find out anything,' said Theodosia, 'it may be our duty to do something, warn somebody. But it's not up to us to obtrude ourselves, to make officious enquiry. Teresa.'

'Theodosia. Theodosia.'

Well, thought Leonard Percival, Lord Canteloupe's Private Secretary, who was sitting concealed in an almost opaque thicket a few feet from the pool, one certainly gets good value from this coppice. These days I only come here (when well enough to walk this far) for a bit of peace and meditation. But in the past there have been many piquant scenes by this pool, and now it is so again.

'Teresa, Teresa.'

'Theodosia.'

Canteloupe, thought Leonard, will be delighted that her ladyship should have such a beautiful young friend to pass the time with. But he will *not* be delighted if either of 'em *should* get any wiser about what is intended for Sarum. There is no reason at all why this should happen: they have plenty to occupy themselves with just now. But it might happen, it just might. And if so . . . oh dear, oh dear. Never mind, Leonard, he thought; don't bother about all that just now; just enjoy what's going on – one thing at a time.

'Teresa? Teresa?'
'Theodosia, oh Theodosia.'

Miserable, thought Maisie Malcolm: miserable as a string of piles. Nobody here, only poor little Rosie: Fielding in Australia, silly old wanker; Marius off for this half Quarter with his schoolmaster; and my Tessa gone to another big house in the country. And of course she'll be going to those more and more. First that place of Mr Conyngham's in Somerset, now this one in Wiltshire, of course she'll be going, so clever and pretty as she is, and you'll *not*, Maisie Malcolm, get possessive and stand in her way.

Meanwhile, what to do with poor little Rosie? There's those Blessington girls, now. Why can't she ring up them? Caroline might be at home and Jakki should be back from that School for this half Quarter exeat.

So at luncheon Maisie said:

'Them Blessington girls, duckie – why not ring them up?'

'Them Blessington girls,' said Rosie, in courtesy and not in mimicry, 'have gone motoring in France with their parents for the whole of Jakki's half Quarter break. They will be passing quite near St-Bertrand-de-Comminges, where Mummy and Jo-Jo and Oenone are living with Jean-Marie Guiscard. I have suggested to Caroline that they do *not* call in there. Mrs Blessington might not be chuffed by Mummy's behaviour with Jo-Jo.'

'Why didn't your mummy have you out for the half Quarter?'

'Mummy gets more stingy every day. She does not consider it worth buying a return air ticket for a stay of only a week. I don't want to provoke her by complaining: for if I am not careful, Mrs Malcolm, she won't even get me a ticket for the summer holidays.'

When everyone was back at School after the half Quarter exeat, Milo Hedley took Marius Stern out to tea at a nearby farmhouse.

'So,' said Milo, 'how was it with Raisley in Norfolk?'

'Very pleasant. We went to lots of nice places.'

'He gave you your instructions?'

'Yes. They don't apply just yet. I don't think they'll *really* apply until after I've been out to Jeremy and Fielding in Australia.'

'That's all fixed then?'

'Yes. Jeremy's sent a ticket to my lawyer.'

'And Raisley said it was all right?'

'Of course.'

That lovely evening at Castle Acre, thought Marius: Raisley had given full permission then. I suppose, thought Marius now, that I don't really need his permission; but I am happier, much happier, to have it. Anyhow, everything is all right.

'The trouble is,' said Milo, 'that it isn't all right – not any more.'

Milo passed over the tea table a cutting from that morning's *Telegraph*. Marius didn't bother much with the newspapers, since they were largely about malingerers, politicians and psychopaths, so he had not yet seen this.

135

said the *Telegraph*. It appeared that the Honourable Jeremy Morrison, second son of Lord Luffham of Whereham (formerly Peter Morrison, MP) and the travelling evangelist of the 'Back to Mother Earth' movement had been accused of public importuning for sexual purposes in Adelaide . . .

. . . 'I'd like to oblige an Honourable, sir,' the Serjeant-Trumpeter had said to Jeremy, 'but I'm a married man.'

'She'll never know.'

'That's not quite the point, sir. I love her and I can't let her down.'

'Five hundred quid.'

'Don't talk like that, sir. It dishonours us both.'

'I have to have this. Done to me. Serjeant.'

'There's a bar, sir. The Oxoxoco. That'll be the place you want. So one of the lads was saying.'

The Serjeant-Trumpeter was a very kind man, and he actually walked with Jeremy to the Oxoxoco, though he refused to come in. What neither of them yet knew was that there were two bars: the Oxoxoco, which was where they had now arrived and was perfectly respectable; and the Oxoxoco Bottle, of which 'one of the lads' had spoken and which wasn't. So when Jeremy announced to a post office employee (whose wife had gone to what she called the toilet just before Jeremy came in) that he'd got a nice bit of oxtail to offer, the man was at first puzzled, then, when treated to translation, furiously indignant, and was of course made all the more so by Jeremy's plush pommy accent . . .

. . . 'Mind you,' said Milo to Marius, 'he'll be let out on bail. But I don't think, in all the circs, that he'll want you to join him.'

'I could always . . . go about . . . with Fielding Gray.'

'I imagine Fielding Gray will come home pretty sharpish. He's not the chap to stand by a chum in a nasty jam – he's a natural passer-by on the other side. He'll produce some immaculate excuse, and glide away from Jeremy as smooth as a ghost.'

Well, thought Marius, Jeremy had once contrived to glide away from Fielding without much remorse when it suited him; not so long ago either. How rotten Jeremy was: he let everyone down in the end.

'You know what the answer is, don't you?' said Milo. 'Jeremy's got an itch in his arse. They have it, some of them. They do it once or twice, more or less by accident – and then suddenly they're permanently on heat. He'd probably have co-opted you to fuck him pretty soon. Just imagine: those lovely great wobbly white buttocks.'

Marius looked at Milo in interrogation; Milo nodded.

'Rather nice,' said Milo; 'we both enjoyed it very much.'

His tea untasted, Marius crept away from the farmhouse. He felt utterly defeated. The thought of Jeremy, as he displayed and deployed himself for Milo, filled him with sadness. Why had Milo told him? Out of spite, thought Marius, because Milo had sensed that Marius was now the important one with Raisley Conyngham, that he, Milo, was now nothing more than a messenger boy to Lancaster, a pawn where Marius was Knight or Castle or even Queen. But if Milo wanted revenge, he had certainly got it: thinking of Jeremy's fair round face (as it had always been for him), then thinking of the same face distended and squealing in pathic pleasure, Marius passed into the woods which overlooked the valley of the Wey, and sat on the ground to weep.

'One has to remember,' said Raisley Conyngham to Milo Hedley, 'that we are acting for Lord Canteloupe – with no other reward in view than the proving of our own theories and the gratification of seeing them translated into action. And, of course, the satisfaction of obliging an important nobleman, whose orders we must – since we agreed voluntarily to come into the thing – absolutely obey.'

Conyngham sat down on a central pew of Guildford Cathedral, to which they were paying a visit of patronizing inspection, and Milo sat down beside him. Conyngham, for some reason, assumed an attitude of prayer.

'Now, God,' prayed Conyngham, 'until the other day I had everything planned to allow for whatever course Canteloupe might wish to adopt, for any possible changes of his mind.'

Milo now knelt, the more easily to hear Conyngham's orisons.

'Early in August, God, Your servant and mine, Milo

Hedley, was to go to stay with the Provost of Lancaster once more, ready to monitor or manage any trouble in that quarter. For we have to remember that the Provost is (a) Sarum's grandfather on the distaff side, and (b) Marius's uncle by marriage. Despite his mental preoccupations, he might still get a whiff of what is going on and want to stop it or raise a row about it, thus much discommoding Milo and myself. Milo's job was to be – *is* to be – the soothing and soft-soaping of the Provost.'

'Amen,' said Milo.

'As for Marius,' Conyngham's devotions continued, 'in order to flatter him and strengthen his spirit for the struggle before us, I have suggested to him that Milo's role is a minor and subordinate one and that he, Marius, is the star of the show.'

'Amen, Amen.'

'So the sequence, God, would have been as follows: late in July Marius, assured of my high favour and committed, in a general way, to his task, would have left for a month with Your humble servants, Jeremy Morrison and Fielding Gray, in Australia. During that time certain things would have happened to clarify the situation. Thus, it would have been found out whether Theodosia were pregnant with a boy or with a girl; and, if the latter, what changes Canteloupe might or might not wish to make in his plans. And so on; with the result that when Marius came back to England we should have known fairly precisely how to direct him. Mind you, Milo always disliked the notion of Marius's being absent and out of our immediate control for a whole month; but I thought, and still think, that such an absence would be the best thing possible – always providing that he came home punctually, and there would have been many ways of ensuring that.

139

'But *now* what has happened, O God? Jeremy Morrison has been charged with indecent behaviour and will almost certainly be disgraced before the world; and his friend, Fielding Gray, has predictably deserted him and is on his way back to England. So that no Australian trip is now possible for Marius – '

' – And Your two faithful servants,' said Milo, 'Raisley Conyngham and Milo Hedley, are well and truly fucked up.'

Raisley rose. 'You should never commit blasphemy, Milo. Discourteous language to God is definitely in poor taste and invites retribution.'

'That,' said Milo as he followed Raisley out of the Cathedral, 'depends on what God you are speaking to. Even a moderate Dualist position allows the title to either of Them.'

'And certainly enjoins respect for Both. The object of prayer, Milo, is to clear the mind. Bad manners, to Whichever God, do not assist in that purpose.'

They climbed into Raisley's Renault 30 Turbo-Jet and headed for the Hog's Back.

'In fact,' said Milo, 'your prayers have cleared my mind most splendidly. As you stated, I *was* very much against Marius's trip to Australia. Only now that it cannot come off, do I realize just what problems are posed by its cancellation.'

'Good, Milo. You seem to have absorbed some of God's Grace after all. Summarize these problems for me.'

'This cancellation means that we shall have Marius hanging around for nigh on a month and doing nothing. It means that he will be vulnerable to the interference of time, chance, the approaches of other people concerned, the pressures of waiting, the anxieties caused by random and idle speculation – in short that he could, *could*, sir, become utterly demoralized, instead of being the Marius you hoped for, a nice, calm, relaxed and compliant Marius, home from a gorgeous holiday treat with his favourite Jeremy, rested and ready for what is to come.'

'Bravo, Milo. So in one word, what are we *now* to do with Marius in August? We are into July. The matter is urgent. Speak, O blessed child, with this new insight that God (Whichever of the Two) hath given thee.'

'Could he come to Lancaster with me – to his Uncle Tom Lewlyllyn?'

Raisley stopped the car in a lay-by. He moved behind some bushes and started to piss. Milo joined him and did likewise. The School, on its hill to the south, was in their exact line of fire but of course well out of range.

'No,' said Raisley Conyngham at length, as he shook the drops off. 'I have taught Marius to regard your role as inferior. If I sent him with you to Lancaster, he would start smelling something behind the Provost's arras. Besides,' he said, putting his doings away, 'I do not like the impressions I am receiving of Llewyllyn's Private Secretary, Len. Len, it seems to me, is just the sort of person who might mislead or disorientate Marius.'

'Granted. Will you now favour me, sir, with *your* suggestion. What do you propose to do with Marius for August?'

They pottered back towards the Renault.

'I,' said Raisley Conyngham, 'shall let someone else do it for me. I shall leak a little information to Marius's connections implying that Marius (as they doubtless suspect already) is in rapidly increasing moral danger. They will then fly to his rescue – and I am tolerably certain,' he continued, 'of the solution they will come to, a solution that would in fact make things very easy for us, for reasons of which I shall apprise you later. And even,' pursued Raisley, 'if theirs is *not* the solution I think it will be, nevertheless, since it *is* theirs, they will feel self-satisfied and virtuous and clever, and go about their other business (which is plenteous and absorbing) without dreaming that anything, now, can go wrong with or for Marius. And when people get into that frame of mind,' Raisley Conyngham said, 'they are richly ripe for *Mors Asinorum*, that is to say for Fools' Mate.'

When Fielding Gray arrived back from Australia, since he did not fancy being alone in his house at Broughton or being subjected to the endless and spiteful questions which he knew that Maisie would ask about Jeremy if he went to Buttock's Hotel, he invited himself to stay with Canteloupe, who, though he had plenty on his mind just then, was passably pleased to see him.

Meanwhile, Leonard Percival had received instructions, which had originated with Raisley Conyngham and been passed on through Giles Glastonbury, that enough information be released about the exploitation of Marius to set Marius's friends on their mettle and so bring about the defensive action which Raisley desired them to take, knowing well what it might be and that it would be in any case ill-judged. Leonard, being pretty near neutral in all of this and not really caring what happened to anyone so long as he himself were allowed to linger out the diseased and distressful days that remained to him at the court of Canteloupe, in fact told Fielding a good deal more than his instructions warranted, feeling that he ought to give his old friend and accomplice a fair and proper chance to come to grips with what was going forward.

'Detterling wants an end of Sarum,' Leonard Percival said to Fielding. 'Although Sarum is your son, you will acknowledge, as soon as you see him again, that the world would be well rid of him. If you want a look, see him this afternoon. Since Detterling and her ladyship are at the County Show for the day, you'll have things all your own way.'

'All my own way?'

'Detterling and her ladyship,' said Leonard, off-handedly, 'do not like people inspecting Sarum. If they are not here, they can make no objection.'

'Won't the nurse mind?'

'I don't think so.' Percival looked as if he were about to add something, but didn't.

'So,' said Fielding, 'Canteloupe wants to be rid of Sarum. How?'

'A very nice question. As you may imagine, Detterling is being rather discreet about the answer. Myself, I envisage some kind of plausible accident, unintentionally (on the face of it) precipitated by an innocent and thoughtless agent. That bill might be filled . . . by Marius Stern.'

'Oh,' was all that Fielding could think of to say for the time being.

Leonard had already spoken far beyond his brief from Glastonbury. Now he added a few helpful hints for good measure.

'That little Tessa Malcolm was here for her half Quarter. She's having rather a heavy walk-out with her ladyship.'

'Great God.'

'Her ladyship and Tessa discussed the matter of Sarum,'

143

said Leonard, 'in the lady-birch grove. They surmise that Sarum – Tullius – may not be long for the realms of light, but they don't really know about that and they don't really care. What they do care about, however, is that no one else should get injured in the action. So,' said Leonard, spelling it out, 'if you want an ally to help protect Master Marius from mental agony or moral injury, go to Theodosia.'

'She's been bothered about Marius for some time.'

'But hasn't really known what was planned for him nor what to do about it. If you tell her what I've just told you, she'll go chuntering into action.'

'Why not tell her yourself?'

'Because I don't really give a fart, and because I can't be fagged to put up with her airs and graces. And because she won't come near me in any case. She thinks, quite rightly,' said Leonard, 'that I am old, lame, lewd-minded if no longer lewd in practice, unattractive, drunken and smelly. She can't understand why Canteloupe – why Detterling keeps me on. She'll talk to you – the sensitive and literate Fielding Gray – but she wouldn't listen to me, not if the Archangel Gabriel came down to request it. God knows what she'd do,' leered Leonard, 'if she knew I'd watched her hot luscious games with little Tessa.'

Fielding met Sarum's nurse, Daisy, as she was wheeling his pram in the Rose Garden. When he asked if he might take a look at Sarum, she gave him an odd look and said,

'You're Fielding Gray, the book writer?'

'The same.'

'Then there's something that may interest you. Come along.'

She wheeled the pram out of the Rose Garden and along the stream towards the grove of lady-birch. As it happened, Fielding had been that way a few months before, on a walk on Christmas Day afternoon with Leonard Percival and Giles Glastonbury, the latter of whom was his fellow guest in the house for Christmas.

'We used to come here sometimes.' said Daisy, 'when her ladyship – the first one – had just had Sarum and was still feeding him. She used to sit in here by the pool with her friend Jo-Jo Guiscard and feed Tully in front of her. It excited them both,' said Daisy in a matter-of-fact way.

She lifted Sarum out of the pram and carried him into the grove, by the secret entrance which Fielding and Glastonbury had been shown by Leonard at Christmas. Sarum, examined closely, was less horrible than Fielding had feared. He had slightly pointed ears, a snub nose – so snub that it was almost flat – wrinkled cheeks and a tuft of bristling hair on the crown of an otherwise bald scalp. He also had a sort of fungoid down on his chin and jaw.

'He can't talk and he can't walk,' said Daisy, 'but other things he can do.'

She squatted on the grass by the pool and began to undress Tullius. When she had finished, Tullius crawled fast to the pool, lurched into it, and began to swim round it.

'He loves bathing in this pool,' Daisy said; 'perhaps it's because his mother liked it so much. We're Baby's baby,' she sang out to Sarum. 'It's splendid exercise for him too,' she said to Fielding.

While the naked Sarum was crawling into the pool, Fielding saw that below the neck he was perfectly made.

He might be, perhaps, just a shade short and thick in the calves, but only if one looked very critically.

'Why can't he walk?' Fielding said.

'I don't know. He just never has.'

Now the girl was taking off her own clothes.

'I bathe with him,' she said. 'He likes that. You should too. You're his father, aren't you? I've picked that much up. You should hold him, mould him, love him, fondle him.'

She had a little line of gold hair between her large but very firm breasts, and another line from her navel down to her generous ginger triangle, which was fluffy, Fielding now saw, not wiry. Her calves, like Sarum's, were perhaps a shade short and stout. Her thighs were very white, with occasional brown moles.

Fielding started to take off his own clothes. This was a kind of ritual, he told himself, an *agape*. He was Sarum's father; this girl, Daisy, the child's only real mother: they were cleansing themselves and each other *en famille*. He was suddenly reminded of a Japanese picture he had once seen. The males of the family were bathing with the females: father, son, mother and two little girls. The father had a prominent erection, the son a creditable imitation.

'They think of these things differently,' Max de Freville had explained, many years ago. 'It is the father's duty to make sure that the son is properly equipped and reacts in the normal way to elementary endearment, which the mother will have been told to lavish on him. The two girls are there to observe, and to learn from, what is now about to happen. Very soon the man will fuck the woman, probably from behind, *a tergo sed non per anum*. At the same time they will both help the boy to masturbate.'

'No joy for the girls, you say?'

'Not this time round. When they are older, perhaps. Female masturbation is very common in Japan – often performed in a rocking chair with a couple of marbles clicking up and down in the vagina as the girl rocks – but it is discouraged in the immature, lest it cause disfigurement.'

'But the boy is not mature either.'

'If you look very carefully you will see a tiny wisp. In any case it doesn't matter. The only effect pre-pubertal masturbation can have on the male anatomy is to enlarge it – which in males is desirable, at any rate up to a point.'

And so now:

'You know what we have to do?' said Fielding to Daisy.

'Yes,' she said. She lifted Sarum out of the pool and crawled out after him. Fielding followed.

'Yes,' she said; 'I know what is to be done.'

She settled Sarum on the grass, supine beside her, and at once opened her thighs for Fielding, who, watching her hand as it gently kneaded his son's enormous (by comparison with the rest of him) little prick, was stiffened by a spurt of desire such as he had not felt for many years.

'We come here often in the summer,' said Daisy, 'your son and I. Tullius will grow up into a fine boy. Look.'

Once again, as he lowered himself into Daisy, Fielding looked. Oh yes: a fine boy. Lovely, well-made limbs. A perfectly arched penis, the foreskin sliding slowly and easily back under Daisy's kind and careful fingers. A fine boy of nearly four years: unable to walk or talk, with a beard of sorts on his chin and the face of a sexagenarian satyr bacchant.

* * *

147

Later on, Fielding escorted Daisy and Sarum back from the grove to the Rose Garden.

'I'm very grateful to you,' Fielding said to Daisy.

'I enjoyed it too.'

'I meant rather . . . that I am grateful to you on behalf of Sarum, of Tully. Of my son. You are giving him the one kind of pleasure he can ever know. What you do for him . . . is the only thing that makes him in any way aware. His only link with humanity.'

'Let's not get too solemn about it,' Daisy said. 'I love this little boy and I like to please him. As things are, *that* . . . that and the swimming . . . is the best way I know.'

'We are saying the same thing. Do you think . . . that we might meet again while I am here?'

'That,' said Daisy, 'must be as God wills it.'

As Leonard Percival watched the pram trundling back along the stream towards the Rose Garden, he thought:

I should have known she'd take him there. I should have thought of that earlier, and got myself down there to see and hear what went on. But this ulcer . . . I wonder what view he is taking of Canteloupe's plans for Tully Sarum. The whole thing would be so simple, if only Sarum weren't the heir-apparent to the Marquisate. If he weren't the heir, he could just be left in the care of that nurse (or another) for the rest of his life. She could keep him clean and see to his needs. There is plenty of room in this place for a dozen like him. But Canteloupe never could, never would own to such a one as his heir; and

Fielding Gray of all people will see Canteloupe's point, even though Sarum is Fielding's own son.

What to do, Leonard? he apostrophized himself. Only one answer, the old answer: just sit still and let the thing go on.

Fielding stayed on with the Canteloupes for some days. God did not, apparently, will that he should have any further meetings with Daisy and Sarum, both of whom seemed to have vanished. He did not broach the subject of Sarum either to Canteloupe or to Theodosia, partly because he himself had yet to form a definite opinion about Leonard's disclosures, and partly because it seemed ill bred to raise a subject, which must be (to say the least) unattractive to them, under their own roof.

Fielding did wonder whether he should attempt to pass a warning about Canteloupe's plan to Daisy. He had not done so during their previous meeting, as it had been his view that one did not discuss important matters with servants (or anyone else, for that matter) until one had known them at least ten years. On later reflection, he decided that this was still his view. In any case, he did not see Daisy; therefore he could give her no warning without passing a written message, and to attempt to do so would excite comment and suspicion in his hosts.

And so, after attending with Canteloupe a few quite agreeable race meetings at Bath and Newbury, he went on his way towards London, decided *en route* that he still could not face Maisie in Buttock's Hotel, and cut across country through Bletchley and Stony Stratford to Stamford, where he took chambers at the George. By this time it was clear to him what he would do about the Sarum business: he must of course (as he always did) land all responsibility for decision and action on somebody else more willing and therefore more competent to bear such burdens, and in this case the ideal correspondent was now less than an hour's drive away.

Carmilla Salinger, sitting in her drawing room in Lancaster College, was not at all pleased to see Fielding Gray, who was walking down the south wall of the Chapel, heading straight for her own staircase. Tiresome, this. For one thing, she expected Richard Harbinger to arrive from London in under an hour's time, and for another she had noticed that Fielding seldom arrived anywhere, these days, without trouble and misery in his train.

And so, of course, it was now.

Having told Fielding that she could only give him thirty minutes, she spent the first ten of them listening to his account of how Jeremy had publicly and irremediably blackguarded himself in Adelaide and the next five being treated to a plausible apologia to the effect that there was nothing Fielding could have done about it all without making matters much worse for both of them.

Having thus, so to speak, buried her old lover, or at least scraped him under the carpet, Fielding proceeded to talk ominously of Marius Stern, who would fain have been her new lover some weeks back, and might indeed, had it not been for the clinging and rebarbative Harbinger, have got the post. Carmilla was told, as succinctly as Fielding could tell her, what was being cooked up for Marius in the affair of little Lord Sarum of Old Sarum, i.e. that he was to be the agent (or instrument) of Sarum's demise, to some extent innocent or unwitting, perhaps, and certainly not ostensible, but nevertheless first party to a murder. Fielding added that, as far as he could determine from Leonard Percival, Theodosia (whose new connection with Tessa Malcolm he did not divulge) could not bring herself to be much fashed about the death of a monster (albeit one as junior and tender as Sarum), but would certainly deprecate the use and abuse of Marius in the matter.

All this occupied another ten minutes, at the end of which Fielding departed, having taken five minutes less than the time stipulated by Carmilla to put the two balls that were bugging him firmly in her court. Carmilla, feeling slightly faint, decided (a) that there was nothing to be done about Jeremy until an Australian court had passed sentence (for Jeremy now had quite as much money at his disposal as she did if there were any possibility of buying his way out of trouble); and (b) that as to Marius, she would consult Harbinger, whose initial misliking of the boy had now turned to sincere interest and sympathy.

But Harbinger had come, she found, simply to proclaim that he was off. An unexpected offer from an industrial sponsor (pharmaceutical) was to waft him to the small

151

central African republic of Bugari, where a new and incurable disease of venereal origin was reported rife. In return for the permission of the Bugari Government to wander at will in the hitherto unexplored Elang Mountains (in which *Homo Picanthropus* was rumoured to survive) Harbinger and his medical researcher must experiment with a new and likely-looking drug on sufferers from Nim (the natives' name for the new disease) in the more remote regions of the country, where it would not much matter if the experiments went wrong. If, however, they went right, it would be a great relief to the nation of Bugari, 37.431 per cent of whose population was infected, and productive of much prestige and profit to Alchemicals PLC.

Having told Carmilla this, Harbinger announced that he must return to London straightaway, but that a quick suck would be in order first.

After Carmilla had chucked him down the stairs with a neat throw that her sister had taught her, she remembered that she had not had time to consult him about Marius. She also remembered Marius's oblique offer to become her lover and her refusal, which latter had been made on pretty well sole grounds of Harbinger's incumbency. This obstacle was now removed. She could summon Marius as soon as his School Quarter ended. And summon a pack of trouble with him, she thought. She had a lot of work ahead of her this coming summer, and hoped to complete comprehensive notes for a book on diseases of the Eastern Mediterranean during the twelfth century A.D.. Marius installed as lover might make for agreeable and therapeutic intervals of relaxation; Marius involved in a lethal intrigue (as portrayed just now by Fielding) would be boring and, even worse, disruptive.

All of which things being so, Carmilla decided, in the

interests of scholarship, to do precisely what Fielding had decided to do in the interests of himself: she would pass the buck.

'Fielding's been here,' she said to Theodosia on the telephone.

'Is he getting on with *The Grand Grinder*?'

'He didn't mention it. It's my belief that it's stopped with the first half. Never mind. Ashley Dexterside has relented and says we shall do very well out of it as it stands – particularly after that rumpus when extracts were printed in the *Adelaide Angelus*. Fielding says, by the way, that that was the main reason why he had to leave Oz so quickly and come home; but I think he just wanted an excuse to rat on Jeremy – as Jeremy once ratted on him.'

'Jeremy,' said Theodosia with restrained mordancy, 'deserves everything he gets.'

'Well, amen to that, I suppose. But Fielding brought up something else. Marius. And Tully.'

'What about . . . Marius? And Tully?'

Carmilla told her what.

'Leave it with me,' said Theodosia, quite quickly.

'Good. I hoped you'd say that. I've got a lot on this summer and autumn. By the way, Thea, I've thrown out Harbinger.'

'That cunt with the beaver? Good on you, Carm,' Theodosia said.

* * *

153

Theodosia, not feeling quite up to driving herself two hundred miles in the heat, hired a chauffeur-driven car from Avis and was carried down to Burnham-on-Sea on the south coast of the Bristol Channel. She then directed the driver to a jolly little house called Sandy Lodge, which was built almost in the sea itself, where she had arranged to talk with the owner, whom she knew as the aunt of Marius's dead friend, Galahad Palairet: his Aunt Florence or (more commonly) Auntie Flo.

'Lonely?' said Theodosia.

'Not particularly. One or other of the old gang drops in on a condescending visit from time to time. One of them took me to the meeting at Bath the other day. Nice day out, though I don't care so much for the Flat. Whisky?'

'No. Preggers.'

'Canteloupe?

'What do you think?'

'Candidly, no, my dear. I saw Canteloupe at Bath. He was with that one-eyed writing bugger you all seem to know.'

'Major Fielding Gray. It's not him neither, in case you were wondering. I'll tell you soon enough – if it all goes smoothly. Meanwhile, a request. A request with some money in it.'

'Then fire away.'

'Galahad's friend, Marius Stern. Can you feed him, board him, wash him and amuse him for a thousand a week?'

'*A thousand?*'

'I've got plenty, and I want you to have some of it. All right with you?'

'Yes, dear: all right with me.'

'Next thing. There are people who want to corrupt and exploit Marius . . .'

'Fancy his cute little bum, do they?'

'No. They fancy his cute little soul. They'll find out very soon that he's here. He'll probably tell them himself. There's nothing we can do to stop any of that. You mustn't even try. And let him have whatever visitors there may be. *But* – let me know every single thing that goes on.'

'Righty-hoh,' said Aunt Florence, rather dazed.

'He may have good visitors or bad. *Good* are his sister Rosie, her friend Tessa or Teresa Malcolm, Teresa's Auntie Maisie, and his mother – though I don't think *she'll* be coming here from France – Fielding Gray, Jeremy Morrison, if they don't put him in an Aussie slammer. My sister Carmilla. Also good, very good, are Jakki and Caroline Blessington, and their parents.'

'Ivan Blessington of the old Hamilton's Horse?'

'The very one. And his wife, Betty.'

'What a lovely man,' said Auntie Flo, not meaning Betty. 'I'm a bit older than him, of course, but I well remember a party in London where some girl asked him to let her watch him while he had a pee. Some rotten spoilsport knocked on the door of the loo . . . Where were we?'

'Marius's visitors. Now the baddies. Raisley Conyngham – '

'The schoolie racehorse owner?'

' – And his pupil, Milo Hedley. Giles Glastonbury, because he's Conyngham's friend – '

' – Acquaintance – '

' – And my husband Canteloupe.'

'Oh. Your husband Canteloupe? Mine not to reason why, I suppose . . . not when I'm getting two monkeys a week.'

'Reason as much as you like,' said Theodosia, 'but

155

don't ask questions, there's a darling. Await my instructions about Marius's arrival, and do as I ask about visitors. Good, bad or diabolical – let 'em all in, but keep an eye cocked and report on all, especially the diabolical. You'll know *them* on sight.'

'One question I *am* entitled to ask, dear. Is Marius looking forward to coming?'

'He doesn't know he's coming yet,' said Theodosia; 'but I can promise you he'll look forward to it when he does.'

Back in Wiltshire, Theodosia rang up Colonel Ivan Blessington, her friend and business representative, in London. Colonel Blessington rang up his daughter, Jakki, at her School. Jakki sought out Marius Stern as he was leaving the Under Sixteen cricket nets. Marius looked at Jakki with pleasure, as he always did. She usually favoured boys' trousers, long at the heel and with turn-ups; but today, since she had been to extra tuition, she was wearing the Gordon kilt with the Gordon stockings and a dagger in the top of one.

'Want to be kind?' Jakki said.

'To you – yes.'

'To me – incidentally. Also to others.'

'To whom?'

'Palairet for one.'

'Palairet is dead.'

Dead on the Field, he thought; true knight.

'Yes,' said Jakki. 'He had an aunt whom he loved. The aunt wants to meet – Palairet's friend.'

'How do you know?'

'My old Dad used to go racing with her. In the old days. She's a very sporty old lady, Marius. She loved Palairet. She wants to meet his friend – says my old Dad.'

'Then I shall go.'

'Lovely Marius.'

'When? Where? How long?'

'End of the Quarter. Burnham-on-Sea. There's a good golfcourse.'

'I'm rotten at golf.'

'There'll be cricket to watch at Taunton. And racing: Newton Abbot, Devon and Exeter, Bath, Taunton, Wincanton and Chepstow,' Jakki recited.

'Do I just go? Don't I write or anything first?'

Jakki produced a sheet of paper from under her kilt.

'Last day of Quarter,' she said. 'Take the one-fifteen from Paddington. Get out at Burnham and take a taxi: "Sandy Lodge," you say to the man, "Sandy Lodge at the end of Sandy Lane." Take a lot of kit in case you want to stay a while. You'll be welcome as long as you like. No need to write or ring up: just go. After all, Marius, now that poor Jeremy's in such a fix, you've nowhere else to go, my love, now have you?'

PART THREE
The Specialty of Rule

In quo corriget?
Wherewithal shall a young man cleanse his
way: even by ruling himself after thy word.

Psalm 119, v.9

Exactly what I'd hoped for,' said Raisley Conyngham to Milo Hedley, as they sat on a bench on the boundary of the cricket field listening (intermittently) to the School Brass Band which was giving the End of Quarter Concert on the Terrace. 'That old woman in Burnham-on-Sea; quite perfect.'

'Isn't she also . . . quite tough?'

'But vulnerable with it. Rackety, sporty, thirsty, gamy, always short of money.'

(Although Marius had, of course, told Raisley where he was going, he had not told him, because he did not know, that Palairet's Auntie Flo was to receive one grand a week for his entertainment.)

'Even if she does wish to make difficulties,' said Raisley, 'and there is no particular reason to suppose so, it will be very easy to get round her, to get at Marius, to get messages through to him.'

'She may send out reports.'

'What if she does?'

'She may summon . . . Marius's good angels.'

'Marius is pledged to serve and obey me. Upon pain of my casting him out.'

'What makes you think he'd mind that?' sneered Milo.

'Because he is my man, Milo, and yours. I reminded him of this at Holkham, where he confirmed his love and allegiance.'

'Vows of love, Raisley, whatever kind of love, are spoken into empty air.'

'I have told you. You will address me as "sir" until you leave this School for good tomorrow morning. You must not get premature ideas of equality or independence, Milo. Just concentrate on your mission to the Provost of Lancaster. Let me take this opportunity of reminding you: your job is to prevent his interfering or enquiring or in any way getting up trouble during the enaction of what now concerns us – in short, to make him forget the very existence of his grandson, Sarum of Old Sarum. You understand that?'

There was a long silence during which Milo discovered that there were some words carved on the crossbar of the back of the seat behind him. Leaning forward and twisting his neck, he read:

JEREMY MORRISON
Placed here by his father, Luffham of Whereham

Thinking on this inscription and on the fate of Jeremy in Australia, Milo let the silence between him and Raisley continue, while the band played right through *Rory Gilpin*, and then at last,

'I think I understand very well, sir,' Milo said, '*now*. So all this,' he went on, making a gesture which comprised the Terrace, the Green and the distant Memorial Chapel, 'all this will be over for me tomorrow. How I have enjoyed it. And you more than all the rest of it . . . sir.'

'Sorry to be leaving?'

'Yes,' said Milo; 'but consoled by the fact that I shall not be leaving you. I apologize for my half-baked and "premature assumptions of equality and independence". And to prove how sincere is my apology, I shall continue to call you "sir" for many moons to come. Anything else, from me to you, would clearly be quite ridiculous. You

162

are my liege and I am your man, as is Marius. All I ask is a small share in him.'

'Ah. Why this sudden retraction, Milo? I could have sworn, for some time since, that you were getting ready to commence Master Artificer in your own right, no longer content to be a mere, albeit confidential, apprentice.'

'I was getting ready, sir. But the fate of poor Jeremy Morrison has taught me humility. "Time and chance happeneth to them all", sir; and the only person I know whose advice might just protect a fellow against both is you.'

'Such flattery, Milo,' Raisley Conyngham said.

'My fee for remaining under instruction as your confidential apprentice and continuing to receive your invaluable advice. For if you do not object, sir, I shall so remain, at least until this affair of Marius and Sarum is concluded.'

'The conclusion of this affair of Marius and Sarum will not mark the conclusion of the affair of Marius as a whole. Shall you not stay for that too?'

'If invited, sir.'

'You are invited, Milo.'

'Daddy says,' said Jakki to Tessa on the train from Farncombe to Waterloo, 'that if . . . if your plans for the hols should fall through, there's room in our car for another. It'll be a squeeze but there'll be room, if you don't bring too much luggage.'

Tessa turned her head and kissed Jakki on the temple.

'My plans will not fall through,' Tessa said.

'I wish they would.'

'Don't be like that, Jakki. This is my best thing ever.'

'With Lady C.? I wish you joy of it, I really do. But I wish, even more, that you could be with us. I dare say,' said Jakki, 'that we could have got up some net practice.' She giggled. 'We could make Mummy and Daddy bowl at us. And Caro.'

'You can do that without me.'

'Somehow, I don't think we will,' said Jakki; 'not on our own. You would have been – what do they call it? – the catalyst. The extra element that changes everything.'

'There's been enough of cricket lately.'

'It's all very well for you. You got your Under Sixteen Colours. Like Marius.'

'Girls' Under Sixteen Colours,' corrected Tessa. 'One must discriminate, I think. You'll get yours next year. Next spring's the time to practise, not now in the autumn, when the season's dying.'

'It isn't even August yet,' said Jakki. 'There's a lovely lawn in the garden of the house we're taking in France, which would have been ideal for net practice. But I dare say you're right,' she said: 'whatever the month, the autumn will not be far off where we are going, and the French would have thought we were potty, and where would we have got the poles and nets? No room for *them* in our car. Besides, I must work for "O" Levels. Only a year left now. What happened about yours? And Marius's? Weren't they meant to be last Quarter?'

'They've been put off till December.'

'Aren't you glad?'

'No. I should like to have got them out of the way.'

'I suppose so,' said Jakki, wondering whether Lady

Canteloupe would allow her friend any time for revision. 'Do you know quite why they've been postponed?'

They passed through Vauxhall, where once the Gardens were.

'The examiners say,' said Tessa, 'that they won't produce the question papers until they get a guarantee from the Board that all "disadvantaged" examinees will get an automatic bonus of fifty per cent on all markings.'

'I didn't think that "disadvantaged" people did "O" Levels.'

'That's the point. The examiners want them to do "O" Levels – and be guaranteed a bonus of fifty per cent to make sure they pass. That will make them equal, you see, to everybody else. So far the Board has refused to give a guarantee.'

'Then your "O" Levels – and mine – may be postponed forever?'

'That is what the examiners – some of them – want,' said Tessa. 'To ruin our education, everyone's education.'

'Except for that of the "disadvantaged"?'

'They won't have an education. Just a fifty per cent bonus in marks.'

Waterloo. Jakki's sister Caroline was waiting for them outside the gate of the platform.

'The man wouldn't let me in,' she explained. 'I found a machine for platform tickets. It took my money and didn't produce a ticket. I explained to the man, and offered him the same money again, but he still wouldn't let me on the platform. I don't think,' said Caroline, 'that he likes girls like us.'

They all looked at 'the man' at the end of the platform, and he looked back. He had a hyena's face with a pimply snout and a beard to hide a weasel chin. He was busy locking the gate and stopping two old ladies from going through to catch the next train out. It wasn't due to leave for twenty-five minutes, the man said. Yes, said one old lady, but they preferred to wait actually on the platform.

'Well, you can't,' said the man. He slammed the gate and slouched away. Luckily another man, who was black, smiled at the ladies and invited them through *his* gate (the adjacent one) and on to their platform that way.

'I think,' said Tessa to Jakki, 'that both those men are "disadvantaged".'

'Most people in British Rail are,' said Jakki; 'let's get moving.'

'There used to be a News Cinema on this station,' said Tessa, as they went towards the taxi rank, 'with reels and reels of news. Auntie Maisie told me. I wonder where it's gone.'

'I expect they closed it,' said Caroline, 'because all the news these days is so horrible or so silly that no one would have gone to it.'

'They had Donald Duck and things as well,' said Tessa. 'How's Rosie?'

'She would have come,' said Caroline, 'but she's had to catch her aeroplane to Montpellier.'

'Off already?' Tessa said. 'I'm sorry to miss her, but I'm glad her mother bought her a ticket. She was worried about that.'

'The house we are hiring in France,' said Caroline, 'is near where Rosie's going to be with her mother. Her mother lives in the chancel of a disused church. Very pretty. Romanesque. Since we are to be so close, I *hope* we shall see a lot of Rosie.'

'Why shouldn't you?' said Tessa.

'When we were motoring through there in the spring,' said Jakki, 'we didn't call on them because we were afraid that our mother wouldn't approve of Rosie's mother living with another lady. Which is what she does. The lady's husband is there too, and the lady's little girl. But the lady cleaves, as it says in the Bible, not to her husband but to Rosie's mummy. Which we thought might upset ours.'

Jakki and Caroline smiled at Tessa. Both took one of her arms and Caroline took on her rather heavy suitcase of old-fashioned leather. For a moment Tessa could hardly bear the idea of not going with them to France; then she thought of Theodosia by the pool in the birch grove and found that she could bear it quite easily.

'But Caroline and Daddy have been explaining to Mummy,' said Jakki, 'about how what Rosie's mother does is quite normal these days and has really always been going on everywhere, only people were too polite to mention it. At first Mummy wouldn't believe this, but then Caro and Daddy showed her a bit out of Thomas Hardy's first novel, *Desperate Remedies*, a bit about a lady and a younger cousin who's come to live with her – and Mummy got the point.'

'Thomas Hardy has always been Mummy's favourite author, you see,' said Caroline. 'She reads *Tess* and *The Trumpet-Major* every year. So when she knew it happened in Hardy, even though it was in his first novel which she's never read, she seemed quite happy about it . . . though she did have rather a funny look on her face. Where's Marius? Why didn't he come up from Farncombe with you?'

'Marius has gone to the West Country,' said Jakki, 'to stay with Palairet's Auntie Flo. Lady C. arranged it,' she said to Tessa. 'I know because I had a message from her through Daddy, and had to pass it on to Marius. Didn't Daddy mention it?' she asked her sister.

'No. Daddy doesn't like to talk about Marius.'

'But he got me to give Marius that message,' said Jakki.

'That must have been because Lady Canteloupe wanted him to,' said Caroline. 'Daddy would do anything for Lady Canteloupe.'

'So would I,' said Tessa.

'We know that,' said Caroline and Jakki. 'Shall you come to supper with us this evening?'

'I think I must be with Auntie Maisie this evening,' said Tessa. 'I am going to Wiltshire tomorrow, so she will very soon be alone at Buttock's. Rosie is gone to France already, you say, and Marius is gone to the West Country. She will be lonely when I too am gone (yet go I shall), and this evening I must be with her.'

'Of course,' said Jakki and Caroline; 'we understand.'

The taxi pulled up where Jakki and Caroline lived, and the pair of them made ready to disembark with Jakki's luggage. All three girls were quietly crying because this was a serious time of parting, and they would not meet again until the autumn, when Jakki and Caroline would return from Languedoc and Tessa from the Enchanted Castle.

Tessa had been wrong in supposing that her Aunt Maisie was alone. Fielding Gray had just come to Buttock's, knowing that sooner or later he must face Maisie and give account of Jeremy, and reckoning on Tessa's being now returned from School to soften Maisie's humour and make up a bit of a party.

They all three had dinner together in Maisie's private sitting room, the hotel dining room being full of people who looked like Esquimaux or Amerindians but were really Orientals (or vice versa).

'Tourists, my dears,' said Maisie to Tessa and Fielding; 'the old place is heaving.' She surveyed a menu which had been especially typed for her own table and included a lot of Tessa's and Fielding's favourite things. 'Very nice to have an excuse to be all cosy and on our own. Besides, those Americans, or whatever they are, would have made a dreadful fuss if they'd seen us having this caviar down in the dining room. They wouldn't have known what it was, mind you, but they would have known that *they* weren't having it, and the whole lot would have wet themselves with paranoia.' ('Paranoia' was Maisie's new word, which she had acquired from Rosie just before Rosie flew away, so that there had not been time enough for Maisie to be accurately rehearsed in its use.) 'And those Japanese, or whatever *they* are, would have been showing their enormous yellow teeth and chattering like woodpeckers. It has happened before, you know, when I've had something special in the dining room all to myself. Well, so long as the travel agents keep pouring the money in . . . I make them pay in advance, you know, even for white people. I see,' she said to Fielding, rippling with pleasure, 'that the Aussies have given Master Jeremy Morrison six months in the slammer. It was in this morning's *Telegraph*.'

'I saw it,' said Fielding, who had anticipated this remark and had his tactic ready; 'and if you ask me, he has only himself to thank.'

Maisie looked at him and nodded.

'All right,' she said, conceding that this must close the topic; 'so there's an end of that until the next time. Six months won't last for ever. Now,' she said, indicating Tessa and rippling once more, this time with pride: 'little

Miss Madam here is off to Lady Canteloupe again, for almost the whole of the holidays. I don't say I shan't miss her, but I'll not spoil it for her. Though I sometimes wonder what her ladyship sees in Teresa.'

Funny, thought Fielding, how naïve this shrewd and corrupt woman could be. Or was she being disingenuous? Aloud he said,

'Theodosia Canteloupe is in need of a friend just now. She likes Teresa (so Canteloupe tells me) because she is quiet and gentle, well read for her age, good at games, and clever.' And for two or three more reasons, he thought, as he smiled across the table, with his twisted mouth, at Tessa: those beautiful round white knees with the ginger down just below them, that angel-corona of auburn hair.

'Well,' said Maisie, 'just as well I've got all those tourists to keep me busy, or I might turn sorry for myself, you know. Rosie went off to her mum this morning and Tessa's going tomorrow, so those nice rude Blessington girls won't be coming to visit, and what with one thing and another – '

' – Here am I,' said Fielding. 'You've got me.'

'And how long are you staying?'

A waiter brought in lemon pancakes, Tessa's choice of pudding as caviar had been Fielding's choice of hors d'oeuvre.

'How long are you staying, Fielding Gray?' repeated Maisie when the waiter had gone.

'Till I've checked the arrangements for the publication of my new book. Then I'll go to Broughton to write the second volume.'

'I thought it was meant to be all in one volume,' said Tessa in her husky voice.

'I got slack,' Fielding admitted. 'And they said that the

first half would do on its own. Certainly, the extracts printed in the press have gone down well – they made a definite stir in Australia. Anyway, now I'm going to write Part Two, which will be very different.'

'Different how?' said Tessa.

'Part One was about the youth of the grandfather I admired and loved: his youth and exploits, and those of his relations. Part Two will be about his old age. And about what happened to his relations.'

'What happened?'

'Death.'

'And before that?'

'The fear of death.'

'And that is what you are going to write about in Broughton,' said Tessa: 'the fear of death?'

'And about the philosophies of those few that did not fear it. My grandfather did not fear it. But I think he secretly feared the manner in which it might come.'

'We all fear that,' Maisie said. 'Rosie had a good quotation in her English last term: "To cease upon the midnight with no pain" – if only we could all be sure of that.'

'In what manner did death come to your grandfather?' said Tessa.

'Swiftly, I think. As a friend. As it turned out, he need not have feared. Others of whom I shall write were less fortunate.'

'So you'll be off at Broughton doing "skulls beneath the skin",' said Maisie, remembering another quotation from Rosie's English; 'and that's the last of you gone for the rest of the summer.'

Teresa looked at Fielding. Something should be done, he read in her look. I'm not going to do it, for I'm going to the Enchanted Castle, into which people like Auntie

Maisie will not (thank God) be permitted to follow me. But something should be done. If you love me, if you love my love, do it.

'Come to Broughton,' said Fielding, resting his hand on Maisie's arm. 'A little sea air would do you good.'

'But all these rubbishy tourists passing through the hotel . . . Who's going to – '

' – Mr Huxtable will manage very well without you. And there's Miss Jackson will help him.'

'Miss Jackson is a snooty and opinionated shrew.'

'But very efficient, which is why you keep her. You are not indispensable, Maisie. Nobody ever is. And you can ring up every day to check on what's passing. Broughton is not a million miles away should there be an emergency requiring your return. Come to Broughton Staithe, Maisie, and see that part of my life and my past which you have never seen. While I write, you can read. You have become very fond of reading, of following up what Tessa and Rosie are reading at School. There is a verandah, looking over the golfcourse towards the sand dunes and the ruined gun sites left over from the war. A scene unspoiled for the last forty years. So you shall sit on the verandah, and every now and then you can raise your eyes to the dunes and the wartime bunkers, and you can say to yourself, "That is where my friend, Fielding Gray, used to wander, when he was a green boy, sick for love."'

Before Raisley Conyngham travelled down to Ullacote he had luncheon with Giles Glastonbury, who entertained him at the Savoy Hotel.

'There's much better fodder at any of my clubs,' grumbled Glastonbury, 'but it won't do for people who know us to see us together . . . now that things are warming up.'

'Will no one know us here in the Savoy, Giles?'

'They're all too important in here – or think they are – to bother with the likes of us. American Jews and oil men, business scum from Japan. They're not interested in an ex-cavalryman and an usher. Oh yes, I know you own a string of horses, but they're all in training for National Hunt, and this lot here wouldn't be interested in anything that didn't fetch a clean million as a yearling. In short, my boy, we're two little blobs of nothing in this place, and that's how we want it.'

Raisley could imagine few men less like a blob of nothing than Glastonbury, who stood out among the runty clientele of the Savoy like an Admiral of the Fleet on the bridge of his flagship. When he said something of the kind.

'But none of them knows or cares who I am,' Glastonbury said. 'If we'd gone to Brummel's, half the chaps there would have said, "There's that brute Glastonbury with that sly little sod, Conyngham, and by God, they look as if they're plotting something." The word would have gone round – '

' – And then been instantly forgotten – '

' – And then been remembered again, perhaps, when certain bits and pieces came floating in with the flood tide at the autumn equinox.'

'Quite the poet today, Giles.'

'Pulses, Conyngham. That's what it's all about. Rhythms and pulses. Call that poetry, if you like. Rhythms in the ocean tides: pulses in the blood of man and woman. For woman, read Theodosia Canteloupe.

173

She's had her fluids tested, whatever that may mean. They say she's going to drop a girl when the time comes. Canteloupe told me two days ago.'

'Is he disappointed?'

'Oddly enough, no. He's rather tickled. Chuffed, as the troops used to say; chuffed to buggery. He thinks that a girl by young Marius and out of Theodosia might be quite something. "The mistake I made over Sarum," he said, "was to bring that old wretch Fielding Gray in on the job. Of course he sired a stumer. But that spunky young Marius . . . It could be a different tale with him getting up between my lady's legs. Not just a girl, Glastonbury: a Princess."'

'Then . . . as regards Sarum . . . we proceed according to our original intention?'

'We do. That is to say, you do. Canteloupe takes the view that if once Tully Sarum were out of the running, a girl would certainly inherit the Barony after his own death and that would be enough for her to do the thing really well. Like a "Princess", to quote his word again. He sees it all as a kind of fairy tale. Anyway, there was never much chance that that poor little beast Tully would get a reprieve, whatever happened. Even if Theodosia had been booked by the apothecary to bring forth nothing but a couple of wet farts, Canteloupe would still have wanted Tully out of the way, and who can blame him? No one wants the Fairy Fella's by-blows cluttering up the senior nursery.'

'Very well,' said Raisley Conyngham, 'I'll set the thing in train. It's simply a matter of presenting the facts in such a way that Marius can respond as we would wish in the first instance, and after that . . . "Now let it work", as Mark Antony observes in the play.'

'Surely things can go wrong in the working? Between

Marius's "response in the first instance" and the right true end?'

'Things can always go wrong under the moon, Glastonbury. The advantage of *this* method is that if something does go wrong, no one will ever know of it. No one will even know that there was anything to go wrong, because events will have followed an entirely normal progression . . . as they will do if everything goes right.'

'But in the former case, Sarum would still be there?'

'Obviously. But no harm done. No alarums, no excursions, no suspicions. Nothing to stop another effort as soon as you wish.'

'I see,' said Glastonbury. 'Very well, Raisley. Pull the switch.'

Marius had a lovely time staying with Palairet's Auntie Flo. He liked her; he was charmed and amused by her house, which, at high tide, was positively in the sea; he enjoyed the race meetings and cricket matches to which she took him (in a chauffeur-driven car, sometimes, which still left plenty of change out of one grand a week): he put in some useful days of work for his postponed 'O' Levels; and he was gratified by the delicious food and drink which, now that there were means to do it and an audience to appreciate it, she put on day after day with never a single dish repeated.

For her part, Auntie Flo, while not exactly loving Marius, regarded him as something very precious, something fragile if not volatile, something wholly out of the ordinary – something to be tended and served, not quite worshipped but satisfied, placated and perhaps flattered (lest of his own will he should leave the precinct and seek another); something, furthermore, to be guarded and secured and protected, lest strange or greedy men should come to steal away such treasure.

And then, one morning after Marius had been at Sandy Lodge nearly three weeks, Captain Jack Lamprey turned up. He was known to both Marius and Auntie Flo as Raisley Conyngham's private trainer, and was remembered by Auntie Flo as a disreputable but not totally unendearing figure from 'the old days'. Although, as being of Raisley's household, he clearly came under Theodosia's category of 'Baddies', he was, she remembered, like all Baddies, to be admitted without question, observed and reported on. Auntie Flo therefore admitted him not only without question but with considerable nostalgic pleasure (Sozzler Jack of Hamilton's Horse), gave immediate assent when he proposed to take Marius out for a walk along the shore, and obeyed her orders from Theodosia by following them along the beach as far as she could with her bare eyes and then with her binoculars (Sozzler Jack had always liked girls, but you never quite knew these days), and carefully entered the time of their starting out and the pace of their progress in her Log Book for Theodosia.

'First of all, laddie,' said Jack Lamprey to Marius as they walked on the hard sand just below the tideline, 'love from everyone at Ullacote. Most of all from Jenny. But as we know, the Governor has his reasons for not wanting you there just now – perhaps not for a very long time – and that is simply that.'

'Is Milo there?'

'For a couple of nights, he was. Then he went off to some college at Cambridge.'

'Lancaster?'

'That's it. Lancaster. Now, laddie,' said Sozzler Jack, 'it's like this. I'm the messenger boy. I've got my message, and I've got it right. You can ask questions, but only if I don't make the thing clear. There's to be no probing, no speculation, no enquiries about ancillary matters. Right?'

'I suppose so.'

'Well, then,' said Jack in his beautiful mellow voice, flowing over his solecisms, caressing his coarseness and making music of his obscenities: 'Raisley says that Glastonbury says that Canteloupe says that Theodosia Canteloupe has had her jolly old juices checked and is going to throw a female. It's not your fault, and Canteloupe is not displeased. He will settle for a girl, but when the popping's stopped he'll probably want you and Theodosia to try again for a boy.'

'What about Sarum?' Marius said.

'Sarum is no part of my message. My message is that a good girl will be good enough, but a boy will be better, because a boy can be a Marquess and a girl can't. A girl can only be a Baroness – '

' – So what about Sarum? – '

' – I told you at the start. No enquiries about ancillary matters. Where was I?'

'A girl can only be a Baroness.'

'Righty; but Canteloupe will happily settle for one, provided it's got a handsome head, two shapely arms and legs, and its quim is in the right place. If it hasn't got all those things, or if it's just an ugly little mandrake, you and her ladyship go jig-a-jig all over again, hoping for better luck next time out.'

'And even if it – if she – is perfect, he may require me . . . to lie with Lady Canteloupe once more, in hope of my begetting a boy?'

'Pompous way of putting it, but you seem to have the point.'

'End of message?'

'Not quite, no.'

'So there *is* something about Sarum?'

'Fuck Sarum. That is to say, as I've already told you twice, no, there's nothing about him. The rest is about your little chum, Tessa Malcolm.'

'Oh? And where does she come into all this?'

'You well may ask. She's fallen for the Marchioness. The Marchioness has fallen for her. They've got a real pash going between them. Which could mean problems, if you think about it carefully, when it's time for you to have it off again with Theodosia.'

'And what does Theodosia think about it all?' said Marius.

'Nobody's asked her. She's happy for the time being with little Tessa – by the way, she always calls her "Teresa" – who stays with her twenty-four hours of every day. She doesn't seem to be thinking of much else.'

'The child?' said Marius. 'The child she's carrying? She must be thinking of that.'

'Apparently she's behaving . . . as if she and Tessa are in some way bearing the child together. Tessa goes along with that.'

Marius, tall for his age, halted and looked out over the Bristol Channel. Stumpy Jack, whom Marius topped by a head, lurked beside him. Eventually Marius said,

'If Tessa can comfort my lady, can in some sense ease her burden by sharing it, then that must be to the good. But what will happen in September . . . when Tessa returns to School, as return she clearly must, and leaves Theodosia alone?'

'Search me,' said Jack. 'But that comes under the

heading of ancillary matters. No speculations allowed there. All I'm told to do is to warn you that Tessa and the Marchioness have got this crush on each other, and that this might make a difference after the child is born and you are required, as you may be, to go again and lie, as you have put it, with her ladyship. You've got to start thinking about how to manage it now. The idea is, you see, that since you've always been close to Tessa/Teresa and she to you, they might . . . let you come in with 'em now and again . . . so you could get the trick done that way. Anyhow, you're to start thinking about it now.'

'But all that is months away, sir. What is to happen meanwhile?'

'Raisley thought you might ask that. You really know the answer for yourself, he said, but if you did ask, I was to issue a reminder: do nothing at all off your own bat; just let whatever happens happen. The Governor was particularly strong on that: you're to sit still, he says, and let the thing go on; if you're needed to take a part, you'll know it quick enough.'

Jakki and Caroline Blessington walked in the woods near St-Bertrand-de-Comminges (ilex and fagus) with Rosie Stern and little Oenone Guiscard.

'When you are here,' said Jakki to Rosie, 'Oenone's mother puts Oenone in your care so that she can give all her time to your own mother. Who takes care of Oenone when you're not here?'

'They all do, I think. Jo-Jo Guiscard, her husband, my mother. They take it in turns.'

'They think Oenone is a nuisance,' Oenone said. 'They are not unkind, but they think she is a nuisance. Oenone is glad that Rosie has come.'

'And Rosie is glad,' Rosie said, 'that Jakki and Caroline have come.'

'Tomorrow,' said Caroline, 'Daddy is driving us into the mountains. Want to come?'

'Is there room?' said Rosie politely.

'Mummy and Daddy in the front,' said Jakki; 'us three with Oenone in the back. Couldn't be nicer.'

'Nicer, nicer, nicer,' echoed Oenone as she ran on in front across a clearing.

'How long is there,' said Rosie, 'before the archangel comes with his sword?'

Jakki took a while to interpret this. Then she said:

'We are here for six weeks. Daddy will have to go back to London, to attend to his work for Lady Canteloupe and Carmilla Salinger – in your father's old publishing firm, Rosie – after three or four weeks. He will leave the car here with Mummy and us. So perhaps, when the time comes for us to drive home (we shall take it very easy), you can return with us.'

'And Oenone,' said Oenone, scampering back towards them.

'I think,' said Rosie carefully, 'that Oenone must stay here. But that is weeks away,' she said, gathering Oenone's head to her belly as Oenone's face crumpled; 'we have no need to think of that. Not yet.'

'Not yet,' echoed Oenone, breaking away from Rosie, 'not yet, not yet, not yet.'

* * *

Milo Hedley walked with Provost Llewyllyn in the Provost's Garden at Lancaster.

'Why is it,' said the Provost, 'that no one will let me see my grandson, Sarum? He came here some years ago to be christened in the College Chapel. There was some fool of a Bishop, I remember, who would talk modern slop at the Font instead of the proper words. In the end I baptized the child myself. He shat himself, so I stripped him and dowsed him. Total immersion . . .'

'I wish I'd been there, Provost,' said Milo, meaning it.

'But no one has brought him here since,' Sir Thomas went on; 'and no one has invited me to go down into Wiltshire to see him. My own daughter's son. And now my daughter is dead, and I am lonely – '

' – Len is here with you,' said Milo. 'I am here.'

'Why do the others not come? Carmilla, Piero, Nicos, Ivor Winstanley and Greco Barraclough.'

'They are all away for the long vacation,' said Milo, lying, knowing that they did not come because of their distaste and even loathing for himself.

'Jeremy Morrison?' whimpered the Provost.

'He is in Australia.'

'Fielding? Fielding Gray? Ah, but of course he went to Australia with Jeremy.'

Milo let this assertion stand. It was, after all, true as far as it went.

'But at least,' whinged the Provost, 'they should let me see my grandson. Sarum. Tullius. Sarum of Old Sarum. I christened him myself, you know.'

'I know, Provost.'

Milo settled the old gentleman on a bench. The Provost pointed happily to a name carved on the crossbar of its back:

JEREMY MORRISON
Placed here by his father, Luffham of Whereham

'I knew him in the old days,' said the Provost. 'Luffham of Whereham, I mean. Peter Morrison, we called him then. He asked if he could put this in my Garden.'

The Provost slept. Len came through the roses.

'He is hankering,' said Milo, 'to see Sarum.'

'He does sometimes. This is the first time for some months. It won't last, this hankering.'

'Good. He can never see Sarum. Not now.'

'I suppose not,' said Len easily.

'In India there are not only Untouchables, there are Unseeables,' Milo said. 'Sarum is Unseeable.'

'If you say so.'

'I do.'

'Then I shall make sure,' said Len, 'that the Provost does not see him. In any case, he is not fit to travel.'

But he could become so again, thought Milo; and he could insist on going down to Wiltshire whatever Len might say: after all, he is Provost of Lancaster still. So my task is now clear. I must soothe away this hankering, that the Provost may stay happy in his Garden.

I should talk to Theodosia, thought Marius. He put down Page's edition of the *Georgics* and looked from Auntie Flo's verandah out over the sea. She is bearing my child; she may be required to do so again; I should see her, so that we may talk to one another in our own voices.

182

But I am contented and well occupied here. Tessa . . . Teresa . . . is taking care of my lady.

I should see Thea. Human eye to human eye.

I have work for my exams in December (if they take place). Tessa is taking care of Theodosia. Any question of my getting another child on her must be delayed for months. After all, Raisley Conyngham says I am to sit here and wait and do nothing; Raisley says that when I am wanted I shall know it.

Jeremy Morrison sat caged behind the wire netting that covered the long first-floor verandah of the infirmary in the Kelly Gaol near Adelaide.

The civil authorities, wanting no present embarrassment nor future recrimination over the delicate matter of dealing with the internationally famous son of a distinguished and much respected English Peer of the Realm, had reached a compromise. They had overruled a self-righteous minority among them that wished to stage the 'Pom-Humiliation' of the century and made a bargain with Jeremy and his lawyers. The evidence against Jeremy, the authorities said, was ruinous and overwhelming, and could be neither refuted nor suppressed: but let Jeremy plead guilty and claim in mitigation that he was unbalanced and badly tired after his demanding progress through the Orient, and the trial would be reduced to a formal minimum, while Jeremy himself would be let off with a light sentence of which he would serve only half, and that half (on grounds of chronic ill health) in a private ward of a prison infirmary, where he would be allowed to read and write as and when he chose, to conduct his private correspondence and his public affairs (such as these still were), and would also be privileged in the matter of food and drink.

So now, here he was, in the fourth week after sentence had been passed upon him, with some two months still before him in which to contemplate his future.

He had once told Fielding Gray that if ever he were disgraced he would simply retire to his Manor at Luffham and there lead the good life that Horace had led on his Sabine farm – rural, scholarly, unambitious and self-indulgent. But he knew now, as indeed he had known when producing this idyll to Fielding, that his life and tastes had become too various and too hectic for him to be satisfied with the pursuit of literature in bucolic peace. He needed public action; he was also a figure of crimson scandal. Thus the action, for a time, must perhaps be private, but action he must have – and here, delivered to him by a vast androgynous warder)'Maily-waily, Jeremy tweetie') not fifteen minutes before, was a very sensible letter from Carmilla Salinger turning precisely on the problem of how and where he should launch himself on leaving quod.

'Fielding says you've turned yourself into an insatiable pathic,' wrote Carmilla.

You'd better chuck that, Jeremy. American friends tell me there's a nasty shock coming to buggers very soon, which could mean 'matters against you for your life' if you go on getting yourself screwed. So just stop it. Quite apart from anything else, it's damned undignified.

So how are you to occupy yourself when they let you out? A suggestion. My horrible ex-lover, Richard Harbinger, has been employed by a firm called Alchemicals PLC to explore some vile little African country on condition he tries to push some

184

medical muck they want to sell there. This gave me an idea: our printing-cum-publishing firm (mine and Thea's, Canteloupe's and the Sterns') is now to sponsor a journey of exploration, a journey by you, if you will, in some region of your choice that must be obscure, perilous, uncivilized and remote, on the following conditions: that you are prepared to receive maximum publicity – you in conjunction with our firm – both before you go and after you return; that you (being as rich as you are) contribute one quarter of the cost; and that any book you later write about your expedition is to be offered, in the first place, to us.

We are in this for advertisement, Jeremy: we are turning patrons of exploration as other firms turn patrons of steeplechasing or yachting. As a matter of act, I first conceived the notion as a way of getting Richard Harbinger off my back, but Alchemicals caught him in the nick of time, and now the job's on offer to you. The good thing is, you see, that this rumpus in Australia is just the kind of thing we need to lend colour to the publicity: in most cases a conviction for soliciting to sodomy would be the last thing your employers would want; but in this case you can be puffed as the Byronic Sinner seeking God (or the Devil) in his Wanderings, or even as Roland crossing Wilderness and Desolation to the Valley of the Dark Tower, which may contain anything from the Grail to the Witch of Endor. All this, as you may imagine, suits us down to the quick.

Think it over, cheri. I don't want you to end up in some lousy hole as a diseased and jelly-bottomed catamite. You were – in a way you still are – My Man (the best of the bunch, Jeremy, and I mean that) and I would wish (as would Theodosia) to be made proud of you.

Best love

from Carmilla.

PS Do you remember that time we made each other come in Ely Cathedral? What a scream – quite literally for my part.
xoxox C

PPS This thing I'm proposing would enable you to get out of the 'Mother Earth' circus before you're rumbled as a fake (as well as a woofter) and without further explanation.
Carm.

Well, thought Jeremy, as the huge warder brought in his luncheon on a tray ('Din-dins, duckie pie'), there are many worse roles than Childe Harold or Lord Jim.

Some days after Sozzler Jack Lamprey's visit, Marius began to grow restless. It was all very well being told to sit and wait; even though a fellow was well occupied with Virgil while waiting, and well entertained in the intervals of study, a time came when he started to feel nervous. He needed, at the least, somebody to confide in (up to a point) and somebody to boast to. Auntie Flo was handy for both purposes.

'You know that chap that called the other day?' Marius said to Auntie Flo as they sat and watched Botham of Somerset showing off against the mediocre and charmless bowling of Dilley of Kent.

'Jack Lamprey? I've known him for aeons. Crooked little brute but a fine trainer – if he can keep sober.'

'He mostly does, these days. If Raisley Conyngham gets rid of him, there's nowhere left for him to go. They both know this perfectly well, so Mr Conyngham takes advantage and often uses Captain Jack as a kind of running fag . . . like the Monitors and Bloods at our School use the bubs.'

'I thought you didn't have fagging any more.'

'Not officially,' said Marius. 'But most of us are pre-pared to fag for someone we admire – given a decent tip, of course.'

'*You* don't need tips.'

'Others do, and I must do as they do . . . Mr Conyngham was fagging Captain Jack the other day – sending him here to deliver messages.'

'Indeed,' said Auntie Flo, feigning indifference.

'Messages about Theodosia. She's pregnant, you know.'

'I do know.'

'I think she's unhappy about something. I think I'd better go to see her.'

'What business is Lady Canteloupe of yours?' said Auntie Flo, divining the answer.

'She's a sort of partner in our publishing firm – Salinger, Stern and Detterling. My father and Detterling started it years ago, and then the Salingers came in with their money. So you see, Theodosia is more or less my partner.'

'By Detterling you mean Canteloupe. He's a partner too,' said Auntie Flo, who had done a bit of homework about the *personae*, that is to say the public masks, of those whom she might encounter in her role of Marius's custodian. 'He is also Lady Canteloupe's husband. If I were you, Marius, I should leave her to Canteloupe. Strictly his business.'

'Canteloupe is not the father of her child.'

'So she told me.'

'Then someone else . . . someone other than Canteloupe . . . should go to her now.'

'She expressed no desire to be visited. Are you happy, Marius, at Sandy Lodge?'

'I've never been happier,' said Marius truthfully. 'Thank you, Auntie Flo.'

'If you want to thank me, just stay there with me.'

'I'd like to. But I'm jittery.'

'Why?'

'Something has to happen sooner or later.'

'Yes. You will have to go back to School. Be content until then. Don't spoil this good time by hankering.'

'Something will spoil it. Something always does.'

'Then let it not be you.'

'You are right. Thank you again, Auntie Flo.' He leaned across and kissed her on the cheek. She remained motionless save for a quick flicker of pleasure under one eye. 'I promise I will not hanker any more,' Marius said. 'Zowie, did you see that? Botham has the devil's own luck.'

'He also has great strength and very swift reactions. In a few years he will have neither. He will need to improve his method. He looks to me too conceited to acknowledge the necessity.'

Sharp old bird, thought Marius. And just think of all those winning tips she's given me at the races – at long odds, some of 'em. One should always listen to Auntie Flo. So of course I shall obey her and not hanker after seeing Theodosia. I'll stay put in Sandy Lodge and like it, as she recommends. After all, Raisley Conyngham's instructions are the same, and he would be very angry if I tried to diverge from them. Sit still, says he; sit still, says Auntie Flo. And sit still, therefore, I shall; since they both say the same. The only thing is . . . that Raisley Conyngham does not mean quite the same as Auntie Flo.

Fielding Gray read through his first (manuscript) draft of Chapter II of *The Master Baker*, the companion volume to *The Grand Grinder*. He found the work passable, altered the final sentence so that it now ended in a heavy and conclusive monosyllable, and looked across the ninth fairway of the Broughton Staithe golf links towards the sand dunes. There, on a deckchair in the shade of the rear wall of a ruined military latrine, sat Maisie. She had a small blue volume on her lap, almost certainly the World's Classics edition of Trollope's *The Way We Live Now*, which was one of Tessa's set books for her postponed 'O' Levels. Under her rump and out of the sun was a string bag which contained (as Fielding reckoned from Maisie's conversation at breakfast) G. M. Trevelyan's *English Social History*, an early novel of A. S. Byatt, the latest number of *Private Eye*, which had come from London in the post that morning, and a volume of essays by George Orwell.

Maisie had taken post on the dunes at half past ten o'clock. There she would sit reading the heaviest of the works she had with her until two P.M., when she would get up and make a round of inspection of the ruined gun emplacements. She would then reseat herself for a brief doze, after which she would probably, Fielding thought, turn to the relative trivialities of Orwell, then take a quick glance at the *Eye*, and at last finish off her day's study with a stiff dose of Byatt, so that she would have something fresh in her mind to complain of when she returned to the house in time for a shrimp tea. 'Why is that lady so obsessed with pregnant women, dear?' she would say as she went through the sitting room to turn on the kettle, or, 'She writes exactly the same as that sister of hers, the Drabble girl, only with all the fun left out.'

For the first few days after they had come to Broughton, Maisie had rung up Buttock's Hotel twice a day; then once a day; then only three times a week, and now she did not ring up at all, or hadn't for the last ten days; she had simply given Mr Huxtable a standing instruction to telephone if anything important were wanted of her. It was beginning to look, thought Fielding, as if she were going to stay in Broughton for ever. He watched Maisie rise and stomp away for her daily round of the gun sites; then rang up the L'Estrange Arms (just in case of their having a lot of August holiday trash in the place) and told the reception girl that Mrs Malcolm and he would like their usual table by the window at half past eight. 'For our usual filthy dinner,' he said softly as he put down the receiver, and thought wryly of the informed and malignant comments that Maisie (as she did every evening) was bound to make on it. Once, indeed, he had suggested that they should take a taxi to the Jolly Vulture, a justly famous restaurant a few miles down the coast; but Maisie wouldn't hear of it: 'When we've got the good old L'Estrange only ten minutes' walk away?' she said. 'I never heard of such silliness and extravagance in all my life.'

Sir Thomas Llewyllyn, Provost of Lancaster College, rang up from his Lodging to speak to Carmilla Salinger in her set of rooms in Sitwell's Building.

'I want to go to Wiltshire to see my grandson, Sarum,' he said petulantly. 'Len and Milo won't let me.'

I should think, thought Carmilla, that the Provost is the very last thing they need in Wiltshire just now; but all the same he has a right to see his grandchild if he wants to.

'Why won't they let you?' she said.

'They say I'm not fit to travel.'

'What does the doctor say?'

'He says I'll be quite all right to go there, in a large slow car, in three days' time – provided I don't have another attack.'

'Very well,' said Carmilla. 'If you go on getting better for the next three days, I'll ring up Theodosia to tell her to expect us, and hire a large slow car, and take you there myself. I don't at all mind Len, if he wants to come with us, but I draw the line at that slimy little reptile, Milo Hedley.'

'But I must have Milo. He's so kind and amusing.'

'*Christ*,' said Carmilla. 'Well, all right, Provost. But if you insist on Milo Hedley, I shall make you pay half towards the car. And the whole plan is *strictly subject* to the doctor's confirming his permission before we go.'

Bugger, she thought as she rang off: just as my work on the Great Pox was going so smoothly; but I won't have that old man bullied by Len, still less by that venomous Milo. If the Provost wants to see Sarum, he must be allowed to, and if the shock kills him it might be no bad thing. To have him decaying like this, in public and on the premises, is boring and embarrassing. Of course it's always possible that Thea or Canteloupe (God knows what *he's* up to just now) will forbid the visit; and very likely that Tom's doctor will when it comes to the point, in either of which cases I can just get on with my work. But other things being equal, he must go if he wants; one must really just let God decide.

'Puffing Dick, the Beggar King,' she wrote on the pad in front of her: 'reputed to have been infected with the Pox just by sniffing the air through the door of a brothel; worth a paragraph as a comic curiosity.' Though come to think of it, she thought, it can't have been at all comic for Puffing Dick, when he was covered with sundry lesions and half his nose fell off. But apparently the Pox (the one

191

Columbus brought back) killed very much quicker in those early days, so perhaps there wasn't time for it to break his nose down first. 'The Chronicle tells us,' she wrote, 'that "in seven brief months there was an end of Puffing Dick."' I wonder, she thought, if a Pox, got in his wild youth, could account for Tom's bad health now. If it had been cursorily and incompletely cured . . . like Lord Randolph Churchill's or Oscar Wilde's . . . it might be making a creeping come-back. God let him die, she thought, before it all gets too ghastly: but even if God would let him, the medical profession would no doubt strive to prevent it, however horrible his case. Perhaps they could call in that man of whom Canteloupe and his friends were often speaking – Dr La Soeur. He sounded the sort to see Sir Tom off quick enough. But hadn't she heard from someone (from Thea?) that La Soeur had retired? Or had lost his taste for the risks involved in flouting the ethics of his profession? Perhaps Len could find someone else? Or perhaps Milo Hedley, whose schoolmaster chum Raisley Conyngham was reputed to be a great greaser of nuts and bolts, would know where to find someone to do the trick? I had better, she thought, be more polite and pleasant to Milo, after all: one never knows when one may need him.

Milo had overheard the Provost's telephone conversation with Carmilla, and rang up Raisley Conyngham in Somerset.

'Three days?' said Raisley. 'Sir Thomas will try to visit the Canteloupes, in order to see Sarum, in three days?'

'That's right, sir.'

'Then let him. Things are about to move, boy. In three days' time it'll be too late for him to be a nuisance. In fact, now I come to think of it we shall have a definite use for the Provost. You may recall that Canteloupe is keen that the whole thing should be altogether *comme il faut* . . . and that he favours the idea of a comely monument.'

'I see,' said Milo; 'what better place for that than Lancaster College Chapel?'

Raisley Conyngham telephoned to Canteloupe.

'Now let it work,' Raisley Conyngham said.

Canteloupe telephoned Auntie Flo at Sandy Lodge.

'Emergency, old girl,' said Canteloupe, who had known her on and off for many years. 'At this season, as you may probably know, I always get up an XI against the Somerset County Colts. One of my side's ill. I thought Marius Stern might come in for him.'

'The County Colts are some of 'em eighteen years old,' said Auntie Flo. 'Too big and strong for Marius to be playing against.'

'Oh no. If he gets into the XI at School next summer – as I hear he well may – he'll be playing against fully grown men, let alone eighteen-year-olds.'

'That is very true, Canteloupe. And he's well developed for his age. And in any case he's a proper boy and can't be coddled. He'd kill me if I turned this down for him. Of course Marius shall play for you.'

'Brava, old girl. We play on my ground here. You and Marius are invited for the nights of the first and second days of the match. Get him here by ten-thirty sharp for an eleven o'clock start on the first day – that's Friday, day after tomorrow. Sorry for short warning, but it's an emergency as I said.'

When Auntie Flo told Marius about Canteloupe's match, he said,

'That's super, oh super. They make a big Festival thing out of this game. People like May and Brearley come to watch . . . But all my gear's at School, in my cricket bag. I brought everything else I might need, but not that. Have we time to go and fetch it before Friday?'

'We don't need to. It came by road delivery this morning. I unpacked it without disturbing you because you were working.'

'Funny,' said Marius. 'I never arranged that.'

'There was a message gummed to the handle, from your housemaster's wife. Someone had told her you might be needing it. Very thoughtful.'

'Yes,' said Marius. He shook his head as if to dispel some doubt and took both of Auntie Flo's hands. 'I hope it goes well,' he said.

'It would be nice for you to do great things in front of May or Brearley.'

'I wasn't thinking so much of them.'

'You know,' she said, 'the Palairets were always keen cricketers. Two of them played for Somerset.'

'You're thinking . . . of Pally? Of Galahad?'

'Not really. He wasn't near good enough for that sort of thing. I watched him in a holiday match last summer.'

'He kept a very straight bat,' said Marius. 'It went up dead straight and came down dead straight.'

'Too straight, I dare say.'

Sharp old bird, thought Marius. 'Come on,' he said to her. 'Come and help me sort my gear.'

'Marius will be coming to the cricket,' Theodosia Canteloupe said to Teresa. 'Shall you mind?'

'Not in the slightest. Why should I?'

They were walking round Canteloupe's pretty oval cricket ground. This was a quarter of a mile from the house, some of which was dramatically visible through the one gap in the ranks of the copper beech trees that marched round the oval. While they walked, Tessa and Theodosia, in easy and elegant step from the gap in the trees, through which they had come, and round the boundary towards the pavilion which was opposite the gap, they watched a chorus of groundsmen fuss and fiddle round the wicket.

'It's going to be fast and true, that wicket,' said Tessa. 'Marius likes a fast wicket. He likes to play dashing strokes off the front foot.'

'I don't think he'll get a very high place in the batting order,' Theodosia said. 'He'll be in a side of far more experienced players. Odd of Canteloupe to choose him. Emergency choice, Canteloupe said; but I should have thought – '

' – Shall *you* mind that Marius is coming?' Teresa said.

'Why should I?'

'You do seem to be rather going on about it.'

'I just said it was odd of Canteloupe to choose him,' said Theodosia, with a very slight edge. 'That old woman, Palairet's aunt, is coming with him. I like her.'

'Does Marius know that you're going to have a girl?'

'I haven't told him. Someone else may have done.'

'Shall you tell him while he's here?'

'Why are *you* going on about Marius?'

'He excites me. He has always excited me. The idea of him . . . and you . . . is almost more exciting than I can bear.'

Theodosia was about to reply when –

'Hullo, girls,' said Canteloupe, approaching them round the boundary. 'Will you please come and help with the placement for luncheon on the first day. The Somerset Colts will be rather – er – out of their depth and will tend to huddle together. We need to sprinkle our lot very tactfully among them, so that they can be at their ease with us. Now: their Captain is called James Dankworth, of King's School, Bruton. He can sit between our skipper, Michael Drewett, and his own headmaster, Hubert Doggart. Their Vice-Captain is a small farmer's son from Roadwater: I'll take him on.'

'I should put me or Marius on his other side,' said Tessa. 'Roadwater's near to Ullacote where we stayed with Raisley Conyngham last spring, so we could talk to him about the area.'

'Good idea,' said Canteloupe smoothly. '*You* for the farmer's boy, I think; I might have something else in mind for Marius.'

* * *

'These are your orders,' said Canteloupe to Leonard Percival late on the night before the match. 'You meet Marius and the old woman when they arrive at ten-thirty. If I know her, they'll be punctual to the second. You pass her on to me and my wife for coffee; and you take Marius straight to the ground for fielding practice. On the way to the ground you show him the secret way into the birch grove, and you tell him that my wife is anxious to meet him there for a private talk, which will otherwise not be possible. Tell him to be there at twelve-thirty on the pip, and be ready to wait if she hasn't arrived.'

'And suppose, Detterling, that he's in the field, or batting?'

'My XI will bat first,' said Canteloupe. 'That is arranged. I shall be tossing the coin, as I am the host; my Captain will win; and he will elect to bat. The wicket is firm, the bowling will be moderate, and I have some of the best amateur batsmen in the West Country. By the time Marius will have to leave the ground for his tryst – at twelve-twenty, say – only two of our wickets, at the most, will have fallen. Probably none. Since Marius will be batting at Number Ten, he will not hesitate to go. What may or may not happen after he's gone is another matter. There are several possible sequences, all designed to meet different contingencies and put Marius effectually in the way he must go.'

While Theodosia and Teresa were getting up on the morning of the match, the telephone started trilling by the bed. Thea listened with a very straight face for thirty seconds and then said:

'So be it, Carm. If he insists on coming, he must be allowed to. But I cannot say I'm in favour.'

She put down the receiver without another word.

'Carmilla from Cambridge,' she said. 'She's bringing Sir Tom to see Tullius. They'll be here late this afternoon.'

There was no helpful comment that Teresa could offer, so she offered none but simply accompanied Theodosia into their bathroom. While she was drying Tessa, Theodosia said:

'I was going to tell you something by the cricket ground, but Canteloupe interrupted us. Canteloupe is hinting that after I'm delivered of this girl I'm carrying I might like to try again, for a boy. He is hinting that you and I and Marius . . . You understand?'

Teresa nodded. Theodosia draped the towel on the girl's freckled shoulders and got into the bath herself.

'And so when,' said Theodosia, 'you said that Marius had always excited you, and that the idea of Marius and me together excited you almost beyond bearing, I thought to myself, perhaps it is intended . . . so. And this was what I was about to say to you when Canteloupe interrupted.'

'Do you want another child? After this girl?'

'No. But I want to please Canteloupe, I want to humour his obsession, although I know very well that it is vile and dangerous. I love Canteloupe, you see.'

Theodosia stood up in the bath. Tessa began to soap her.

'Well,' said Tessa, passing her hands over Theodosia's taut and gibbous belly, 'there is a long time to decide. Little Helen will be four months yet.'

'You are determined on "Helen"?'

'I should like our child to be named Helen,' said Teresa, 'because it is one of the enchanted names. But of course you must choose.'

'Perdita.'

'A sad name. But another of the enchanted ones.'

'Canteloupe says,' said Theodosia, 'that if there is no boy, then Perdita will become a Baroness in her own right at Canteloupe's death. The Baroness Sarum of Old Sarum.'

'But there is already a boy: Tullius, Baron Sarum of Old Sarum.'

Theodosia sat down in her bath.

'I think,' said Theodosia, 'that Canteloupe assumes that Tullius, Baron Sarum of Old Sarum, will be no longer there.'

'Do you mind . . . this assumption?'

'Not any more, if ever I did. My only concern now is with Perdita. With you and Perdita. I have a feeling,' said Theodosia, rising out of the water like Aphrodite *enceinte* and being received into a huge warm towel by Teresa, 'that whatever is to happen about Tullius is very near. There is a look in Canteloupe's eye. But what is important,' she said, 'is that the old man from Cambridge should not see Tully. It will bring him more grief and increase his madness. He thinks that the tree nymphs from the elms in the College Avenue still live, and are angry with him for the destruction of their trees, and so took away his daughter, Baby. If he sees Tullius, he will imagine that here is a further token of their vengefulness and further cause for him to curse himself.'

'There is no way,' said Tessa, 'of stopping the Provost from seeing the child. His grandchild.'

199

They walked into the bedroom and began to tend and dress each other.

'He may be taken ill on the road. Or when he arrives. We can put him off for a day or two by saying that Sarum is ill, or being specially treated for something, here or elsewhere. But sooner or later,' said Theodosia, deftly combing Teresa's little triangle of ginger hair, 'Sir Thomas Llewyllyn will have to be introduced to Lord Sarum of Old Sarum . . . unless one of them dies.'

And so now, thought Marius, the day had dawned, and soon he would come to the field of honour. Marius and Auntie Flo stepped out of the hired Rolls ('Rather vulgar,' Auntie Flo had said, 'but rather fun'); the chauffeur drove silently away to park, under the direction of a sergeant of the Wiltshire Constabulary; Canteloupe and Theodosia greeted Auntie Flo fondly; Theodosia looked at Marius as if she were indifferent but not ill-disposed to what she was looking at; Canteloupe handed Marius over to Leonard Percival; and Leonard Percival told Marius that his kit would be taken down to the ground, where fielding and net practice would shortly commence.

'Good,' said Marius, 'nothing like a little pracker with a hard ball after a month off.'

Then should they walk to the ground? Leonard suggested. Canteloupe and Theodosia and Auntie Flo had disappeared. Yes, agreed Marius; let them walk to the ground.

They started through a lush meadow, Leonard perspiring with the painful effort, and passed a grove of lady-birch. 'Here,' said Leonard; 'this is how you enter; *here*;

and here you must enter at twelve-thirty sharp as a lemon and wait for her ladyship. She may have seemed cool just now but she has things for you in private. Twelve-thirty.'

'But the game – '

There would, said Leonard, be no difficulties about that.

The first ball of the match was bowled as the final stroke of eleven sounded from Canteloupe's Campanile in the south-west corner of the Great Court. The Somerset County Colts opened with two up-and-downish fast medium bowlers, who apparently propelled the ball through the air and off the wicket as straight as any two men in England, but were supposedly (to judge from their respective fields) bowling in-swingers from the pavilion end and out-swingers from the Campanile end – which was known as such because the Dalmatio–Venetian Campanile towered above and behind that wing of the Great Court which was visible through the gap in the copper beeches. The Captain of Canteloupe's XI, much prompted by Canteloupe, had sent in to bat a pair of very serious Minor County men from Devon, who, after playing out the first four overs, looked likely to stay at their blocks for ever accumulating an average of 3.75 runs an over, mostly in singles but with an occasional unobtrusive 4.

Marius, who was to bat at Number Ten and had yet to don armour, sat in front of the pavilion, to the right of the gate and to the left of Auntie Flo, who in turn was to the left of Theodosia, who was to the left of Tessa.

Theodosia listened to Auntie Flo, who was full of memories of 'Loopy' Canteloupe, the present Marquess's cousin and predecessor. No one else in this quartette spoke at all, and none of them looked at each other, for even Auntie Flo, in full spate to Theodosia, kept her eyes straight and almost unblinking to the front lest she should miss a single motion of the cricket.

Canteloupe, meanwhile, was strolling round the ground with Colin Cowdrey and E. W. Swanton. His XI lolled about the seats by the pavilion steps or on the grass at the bottom of them. Casual spectators arrived on foot (no cars allowed on the ground, though there would have been plenty of room for them between the boundary and the beeches). These came by private invitation or in response to advertisements in the local papers or on market hoardings; the guests might procure refreshment free in the pavilion, the general public (by paying) in a commodious tent. Seats were liberally provided, and as time went on the crowd became substantial. Small yokels and other of Canteloupe's vassals circulated with score cards. But with all of this there was no noise, or not so's you'd notice: a little applause, that little muted and educated. A great peace settled on the noon-day green, made yet more peaceful by the chant of the cicadas beyond the beeches. Marius thought of *The Scholar Gipsy*:

> Go, for they call you, shepherd, from the hill.

Several times the line repeated itself in his brain; then:

> . . . Here will I sit and wait,
> While to my ear from uplands far away
> The bleating of the folded flocks is borne,

With distant cries of reapers in the corn –
All the live murmur of a summer's day.

until at last his 'eye travels down to Oxford towers', which, in the shape of the Campanile and four handsome chimneys, flickered through the gap behind the wicket.

As the bell struck noon, Theodosia rose, excused herself to Auntie Flo, and, walking in step with faithful Teresa, departed round the boundary, into the gap and towards the house.

'Can't just be having a pee,' said Auntie Flo; 'there's a perfectly good place behind the pavilion. Tired, I suppose. Nice for her to have that little girl to attend her.'

A few minutes later Tessa came back alone. 'Thea's getting forty minutes with her feet up,' she explained. 'She may even cut luncheon; but she's sent me back as I've got to chat up one of the Colts when they come off.'

She patted the empty seat between herself and Auntie Flo, and looked at Marius. 'I know we've parted,' her eyes seemed to say; 'I know that I've left them and you're still with and of them. But we can be friends, surely. Perhaps you might even want to tell me something and I could say something back.'

Marius rose from his seat; Tessa smiled happily; but,

'I must go for a little walk,' he said, 'alone. I know I needn't bother to pad up till at least five wickets are down, and that I probably won't have to bat at all, but I'm feeling jittery. See you both at lunch.'

But would he? he thought. If Theodosia had important private things to say to him, it might be some considerable time before he was back. The bell struck the quarter. Presumably Thea was even now rising from wherever Tessa had left her and proceeding slowly over the meadow behind the beeches, between these and the near end of the wing visible through the gap. If Marius now walked very slowly through the gap, he thought, and then to the right, round and behind the beeches on the other side, then struck across the meadow and so to the grove of lady-birch, he could enter it by the hidden way which Percival had shown him and either find Theodosia there already or wait for her if she were not. In any case he would not be a second later than twelve-thirty. He hoped that Auntie Flo and Tessa didn't think that he was being either peculiar or unfriendly; but plainly there had been no choice but to leave them, for was it not by my lady's command that he came hither to the grove?

When Marius came through the trees to the pool at the centre of the grove, he found Daisy, the nanny, who was sprawled naked on the grass, and Sarum of Old Sarum, who was also naked and was mounted astride Daisy's left knee, leaning forward slightly and keeping his balance by clasping with his right hand at her pelvis and by clamping his left within her open crutch. Seen from behind, Sarum was an entirely normal and wholesome child; it was only when Marius (as he moved round the pool) began to see the simian and wizened face in profile, and also the grotesque length and thickness, for so small a child, of the flamboyantly curved pego which he was frotting along Daisy's white and mole-flecked thigh, that Marius was reminded that this creature was alien.

'Master Marius,' said Daisy. 'We hadn't expected you. Not but what we'll be pleased if you wish to stay and play with us. Go on, you swim a little,' she said to Sarum. She prised him off her knee and threw him (pego flailing) backwards into the pool. He surfaced quickly, shook his head, emitted something like a chuckle, and started swimming in vigorous circles.

'I has to cool him off now and then,' Daisy said. 'He be a horny little baggage, bain't he just? Sit thee down, honey. Strip, if thee likes. Be free.'

'I think,' said Marius, still standing, 'that Theo – that Lady Canteloupe may be coming here to meet me. Rather soon.'

'Not her,' said Daisy. 'She used to come here with her little sweetheart, that little Tessa. Then, one day, her ladyship sniff something wrong. I were coming here myself with Tully, see, and I spots 'em e'en through the trees, so I does, and I stops and hides. "It's Baby," her ladyship say to Tessa, "Baby, o Baby. She don't like us being here. Not now this child is growing inside me." So they stops their bussing and their goosing, and they comes out past me and Tully and never sees us, and they has no time been here since, so now we comes here, Tully and I, all the live day, knowing 'tis secret – till you've come, young Master.'

'Oh,' said Marius, beginning to have some idea of what was in the summer wind. It's meant to be now, he thought, kindly and naturally, almost unnoticeably, but in any case *now*, in such a way that his going hence shall be easy and agreeable, and perhaps even honourable with it. But what about the nurse? She would surely defend her charge. She doted on him. Well, thought Marius, just let the thing go on. He took off his School Under Sixteen blazer, his white shirt, his white flannels, his shoes and socks.

'You'se got no panters on,' said Daisy.

'We don't wear them with games clothes, you see.

205

Besides, I shall have to strap my box there, when I go in to bat.'

'You'se got a little scar. On the bulb. Daisy do see it.'

'It happened when I was circumcised. The skin was too tight, so I had to be circumcised when I was quite old for it. Very painful. And worse, because there was the slip there's that scar.'

'Daisy will coddle and kiss un better.'

Surely, he thought, she never talked like this before? Cases and conjugations crazily awry. Third person for first. Almost as if she were reverting, from being a correctly spoken and correctly conducted English nanny, to being . . . to being what?

He looked at Sarum's supple little body as it skittered about the pool, and then lay back.

'Daisy will kiss and cuddle un better. See: watch un grow in Daisy's hand. There, my honey boy. Thee 'rt sweet as any blossoms that blooms along the tree, my cherry one, my beamish – oh see un grow so big and beautiful in Daisy's hand. Now is time for kisses, one, two and three, o sweet as all the blossoms that blooms along the tree . . . two, three and four, as sweet as all the blossoms that blooms along the bough . . .'

Shortly after Marius left the pavilion, there was a change of bowling. A small, stooping lad with hooky arms and legs and a long, thin nose was put on at the Campanile end. He took a run of four steps, and sent down a low, shortish ball, which pitched just outside the off stump. The batsman, the more serious of the two serious Devon men, played back carefully – carefully and much too slowly. The ball whipped in, vicious and sneaky, to strike his right pad two inches above the foot. The stooping lad appealed to the umpire, in a voice so low that even the umpire could hardly hear him, and the Devon man was very properly given out.

After a time, Sarum crawled out of the water and up to Daisy and Marius. Curiously but without jealousy or resentment he watched them do what they were doing. Then he plucked at Daisy's free arm. She put it round him and took him to her breast. Sarum closed his eyes and started contentedly to suck. The thing is quite clear, thought Marius as his pleasure began to mount. There is something strange, some sport, some divinity or devilry in this satyr child, this rollicking little noon-day Pan, which has altogether infected Daisy. As he has grown, so, more and more, he has infected her. She has become like one of those nymphs in the paintings of Poussin or Boucher, she has become like a dryad or a minor country-goddess who, drunk with blood and wine and music, frolics with all as the dance quickens, with the little faun or satyr godlings as well as Priapus the Great.

* * *

The stooping lad took three wickets in his first over and two in his second.

'Come on, girl,' said Auntie Flo to Tessa; 'we must find Marius. At this rate he'll be needed to bat before lunch. Where do you think he could have gone?'

'Anywhere . . . in all these trees,' Tessa said.

'You've known him for years. His tastes, his habits. What he's likely to do when he's nervous? Think, girl.'

'I suppose it is possible . . . that his cousin Baby might have called him . . . guided him to her. Theodosia thinks that she is here.'

'Baby? The first Lady Canteloupe?'

Tessa nodded.

'She's dead in Africa,' Auntie Flo said.

'Thea thinks she's here. She always loved Marius. There's a place we might find him, if Baby has been calling him. It's a chance, anyway.'

'Then we'd better buck up.'

As Tessa led Auntie Flo across the meadow and towards the grove of lady-birch, Auntie Flo said:

'We used to come here sometimes in Loopy Canteloupe's day. For picnics. Swimming. The pool was just big enough for two or three together. There was a funny way in – near that stream.'

'There still is,' said Tessa, and began to enter by it.

As Tully sucked on Daisy's breast, Marius saw his way.

'We must both cleave you,' he said to Daisy; 'the God requires. The ritual requires. The boy first.'

Daisy gently took Sarum from her breast. She desisted

from her kissing of Marius, who rolled on one side, agreeably tumescent, to await his turn in Daisy's loins . . . during which, having restored Sarum to Daisy's breast, he would block the child's snub nose with his hand and ensure that the pressure of his own breast kept Sarum's mouth gorged with Daisy's. Thus the boy, dazed, a few moments before, by the piercing spasms of an unripe ecstasy, but having emitted nothing and therefore ready (as Marius remembered so well from his own infantile pleasurings) for instant re-arousal – being enfolded, what was more, in the warm and quivering flesh of others as they drew towards orgasm – thus the boy, recalling delicious frenzy and feeling it rapidly remount, not realizing until it was too late that the flow of his breath had been staunched and his life drained from him, would die on his mistress's nipple, both sated with bliss and sensing its imminent recurrence. Surely a good way, a kind way, to go, assisting his friends in their pleasure, in no wise dishonourable.

But it was not to happen this way. As Daisy raised Sarum and then eased the extravagantly swollen tissue into the centre of the labia between her thighs, Auntie Flo (having brushed violently past Tessa, who tried to restrain her) strode manically round the pool and ripped the child off Daisy's belly.

'O, monstrous! Demon, Beelzebub!' Auntie Flo cried as she looked into Sarum's eyes.

Sarum, sensing the enemy, the spoiler of joy, instinctively knowing that this intervention was not made (as Fielding's and Marius's had been) in order to enhance Daisy's pleasure and therefore his own, but in order to destroy all pleasure at all, snarled and then bit at Auntie Flo's obtrusive face. Auntie Flo, blood spurting, recoiled and dropped Sarum, whose head hit the hard earth beneath the dried up grass before he rolled, heels over head, into the pool.

Auntie Flo drooped to the ground. Marius gazed with disgust at the split nostrils and the blood and mucus which welled and bubbled from the gap between them, then reached his cricket shirt from the ground to mop at the flow. Daisy clambered towards the pool to rescue her darling, who lay unconscious from the blow to his head, prone, awash and slowly sinking in the water. Tessa came at Daisy with a hold which she had learned from Theodosia ('You never know, my darling, when you'll need a nasty trick to help you') and hurled her towards the trees.

'It must be best like this,' Tessa yelled at her. 'Don't you see? Like this it's nobody's fault, and when it's done this horrible curse will be gone.'

But ginger Daisy lay beneath the birch trees, not hearing auburn Tessa.

'Now,' said Auntie Flo, speaking through Marius's bloodstained cricket shirt as though through a mask, 'in a very few minutes one of us must go to summon a doctor and the police. There are a sergeant and two constables near the car park. But first I am now going to tell you all exactly what has happened, after which I shall tell you what is to be done.

'What happened was this. Marius came to this copse to join little Sarum – who, let us remember, is his second cousin – in his morning dip. Sarum, as an infant, was swimming naked; Marius, accustomed to swim naked at his School, did likewise. In this the nanny encouraged him; when he said he had no bathing shorts, she simply told him to strip. To his pleasure and not altogether to his surprise the nurse followed suit.

'As Marius and the nurse dallied together on the grass, Sarum, though a capital swimmer for his age, got into trouble in the water – possibly cramp. When Tessa and I arrived, seeking Marius who would very soon have to bat in the cricket match, Sarum was struggling desperately while Marius and the nanny were so deep in venery on the bank that they could not notice Sarum's situation. I went to save the infant, tripped, and banged my face horribly against a tree trunk – as a matter of fact it's not as bad as it must have looked; a few stitches at the bottom of the nose will fix it. Tessa, having seen me fall, dashed to save Sarum; the nurse, at last awakened to what was passing, thrust Marius from her and, still throbbing in her incipient climax, much disordered by guilt, furious that another should be handling and rescuing her charge as she herself should have done long since – the nurse, I say, went to snatch Sarum from Tessa, causing Tessa to drop the child on the bank, from which he rolled into the pool unconscious from his fall. Tessa went again to save him, and the nurse, in her rage and jealousy and shame, attacked her fiercely, for the while ignoring the drowning boy. As they fought, Sarum died. I managed to crawl over and fetch him out – too late.'

And now at last, briefly discarding her mask, she did fetch Sarum out and laid him on the grass. As Auntie Flo, still bleeding badly (though less), replaced the cricket shirt on her wound, Tessa made a perfunctory effort to revive him by kneeling astride him and putting pressure on his lungs.

He'd have enjoyed that, thought Marius, were he still able.

To the great relief of all of them, Tessa's untutored efforts were futile.

'Too late,' repeated Auntie Flo through Marius's cricket shirt. 'After a time,' she went on, 'Tessa, using some judo hold she had learned at School – '

' – From Theodosia,' corrected Tessa.

'I think, my dear, it would be more sensible – don't you? – to say "at School". After a time, Tessa threw the nurse, who was rendered unconscious. Now, what's the news with *her*?' Auntie Flo said.

Tessa and Marius went to look at the supine Daisy.

'She seems to have hit her head on the bottom of a tree,' said Marius. He picked up his cricket trousers and began to pull them on.

'Sorry,' he said to Tessa and Auntie Flo. 'What with all the excitement, I forgot till now.'

'What with all the excitement,' said Auntie Flo, 'I'm afraid I didn't notice . . . except that your legs are rather too thin. Only very slightly, but nevertheless too thin. Just as well perhaps. If they weren't you would be perfect, and that would be a bore. Where were we? *That girl*. Rather a lot depends on her. She's not broken her neck by any happy chance?'

'No,' said Tessa, who had been ferreting about near and beneath Daisy. 'She's been impaled,' said Tessa, trembling. 'Christ, O Christ, it wasn't my fault. She *did* attack me, you said so, you said that's what happened, I acted in self-defence, Jesus Christ forgive me – '

' – Shut up,' said Auntie Flo.

She came over to Tessa. Still holding Marius's shirt to her face with one hand, she soothed Tessa by massaging her neck with the other. Then she looked at the ground. She saw a picnic chair which had disintegrated in the undergrowth. She bent down, examined the chair, then with a practised movement of her free arm (learned many years ago in QARANC) turned Daisy from supine to prone. Nothing was immediately noticeable. Auntie Flo examined the picnic chair again: the canvas was the colour and texture of a shroud used for a burial at sea; one of the struts that had once supported it had apparently rusted away from the rest, for it was nowhere visible . . . until she saw a bare quarter of an inch of it, which was protruding from the narrow space between the bottom of Daisy's spine and the mouth of her rectum.

'So that's what has happened,' said Auntie Flo to Tessa and Marius. 'An appalling accident as she fell. Nobody to blame. Nobody to blame for anything. Nobody living, that is. And here is what will happen now. Teresa will walk – *walk*, girl – to the car park; she will direct the police here and summon a doctor to attend to my nose. There may even be one on the ground. Marius and I will stay here and wait until the police come, tell them all that happened *as I have just told you*, and then go for some much-needed luncheon. Let us hope that the cricket recommences as soon as possible. I do not see why two such eminently desirable deaths should prevent it.'

The cricket, which had been prorogued for luncheon at one-fifteen (Canteloupe's XI having made 120 for 7 wickets), was in fact resumed at three-thirty, by which time the police had heard the story of what had happened as told by Marius, Tessa and Auntie Flo, i.e. as told by Auntie Flo to Marius and Tessa in the birch grove. They were three hard nuts, Marius, Tessa and Auntie Flo, and there was no cracking any of them. The story was, no doubt, disgraceful: nowhere in it was there the slightest element of the criminal (as opposed to the merely wicked) except possibly in Daisy's neglect of her duties while lapped in lewdness, and Daisy was now gone to a higher authority to answer for that.

Canteloupe was approached by the local rector, who said that the cricket could not decently continue on the day of his son's death. Canteloupe replied that he was not so selfish as to let his own grief spoil the pleasure of others. It was, the rector insisted, not only a matter of private grief but also of public respect, and that not only for Lord Sarum of Old Sarum but also for the dead nurse. Canteloupe riposted that the rector, as an old Blue (Cantab) and a guest invited for the occasion, was welcome to show his public respect by leaving or his good sense by staying. So the rector (who did not have many treats these days) decided to stay, and there was an end of that.

It was, however, felt only proper to delay the resumption of play until the corpses of Sarum and his nanny had been removed from the precincts. There was an annoying delay about this, as the vehicle required for the purpose went *kaputt* in the clutch just as it was leaving the Great Court. Canteloupe ordered that it be towed by some of his villeins as far as the Gate of the Demesne, there to await a replacement; and as soon as it was outside the Gate the first ball after lunch was bowled.

* * *

Soon after play had restarted, the ill-favoured and stooping off-break bowler came on again and took another wicket. Marius, as Number Ten, was now to bat. Things were now very bad for Canteloupe's XI, who had only made 125 runs for 8 wickets in conditions in which they should have been well on the way to 300.

'That fellow,' said Auntie Flo to Marius, as he rose to go to the wicket, 'is only bowling low off-breaks. Poor old Galahad would have played dead straight with his dead straight bat and would have been out in three balls. *You* know better.'

Auntie Flo had been competently patched up by Dr La Soeur, who had come as Canteloupe's guest and had no medical purpose in mind, but was only too pleased to oblige. 'I retired yesterday,' La Soeur said to Auntie Flo (who knew him or at any rate *of* him from the past),' and I've come here for the start of a long holiday. It is significant that the beginning of my retirement should coincide with the first honest and absolutely above-board service that I have rendered for very many years.'

'Rubbish,' Auntie Flo had said. 'You ran a free clinic for the poor.'

'I also used them as guinea pigs. And the clinic to mask another, far less innocent. Don't try to whitewash me, Miss Florence. And if you got that gash by hitting your nose on a tree, I'm the Emperor of Mars. Somebody took a bite at it.'

'No need to mention it?'

'None whatever, my dear. I've no wish to compromise your dignity. But of course my silence will mean that this job isn't honest and above-board after all. I might have known that I've been professionally crooked for too long to leave crookedness altogether behind me.'

Well, thank God it was him and none other, thought

215

Auntie Flo now, as she watched Marius walk to the wicket: if it had been some nosey local GP stitching me up there might well have been questions and complications. None now. I hope Marius *does* know what to do with those off-breaks.

Marius did. He put his front foot down the wicket and hit the ball smoothly and exceedingly hard, with a cross bat but also with the spin, high over mid-wicket's head, first bounce over the boundary.

For the first time that day there was loud and liberal applause . . . applause that was repeated when Marius, after stopping the next ball (a yorker) in his block, hit the third in the same way as the first, but this time a perch plus a pole plus a chain into the copper beeches.

When the last wicket of Canteloupe's XI fell at four-fifteen, the score was 202, of which Marius had made 57 not out, a pretty wretched effort by the team, on such a beautiful wicket, but a brilliant personal performance by Marius.

'And of course,' said Raisley Conyngham to Marius at tea in the pavilion, 'the worse one's team has done, the more gratifying one's own success. You and I must now have a word together.'

Raisley had appeared on the ground while Marius was batting, spoken at some length to Canteloupe, and been presented to Auntie Flo (with whom he had long had tenuous acquaintance through their common interest in racing) as one of Marius's preceptors at School. He had talked to Auntie Flo only of Marius's career at the School to date, his prospects in 'O' Levels and his later chances of a Scholarship to Oxford or Cambridge, and said nothing of the events in the grove, of which he had had some account from Canteloupe that had been based on the collated testimony of Marius and Tessa.

What had happened, though not quite what had been planned, was irremediable. What had happened had happened, could not be altered now, and was in any case felt, both by Canteloupe and Raisley, to be tolerably satisfactory. It only remained for Marius to be, as the military say, 'debriefed' (so that Raisley might anticipate any possible future problems with the police or the press, and warn Marius about them) and then, from now on and for evermore, the thing must be absolutely forgotten.

'I can't talk now,' said Marius to Raisley as they rose from the tea table, 'I'll be in the field.'

'No you won't. Canteloupe has found a twelfth man to go on in your place. The excuse is that the police want to interview you further about this Sarum business. And so no doubt they will,' said Raisley, 'which makes it essential that you and I should discuss it at once. There are one or two things we must get entirely straight – only one or two, thank God, but these we must get invulnerably correct, and we must do so now.'

'I understand, sir.'

'That's my good boy.'

They began to walk round the ground in a casual and friendly manner.

'Item one,' said Conyngham. 'Journalists will approach you. When they do, you will simply say that you have given a full and truthful account of what occurred to the police, and that you must decline ever to talk of the matter again, to anybody or in any circumstance. The journalists will bully and threaten, will whine about their livelihoods or start canting about their duty to the public. Simply ignore them, dear boy, and walk away. They are scavengers; vultures that feed on rotting entrails; banqueters of garbage.

'Item two. You must totally dismiss from your mind, if you have not done so already, the course of action you had intended to follow and would have followed had it not been for the intervention of that old woman and Tessa. I do not want to hear anything about it – your original plan, I mean – now or ever. You will also dismiss from your mind anything and everything you might fancy occurred in that grove except for the version of events which was dictated to you and Tessa by the old woman. That is now the whole truth of the affair and there will be none other.'

'I kept to it absolutely when questioned by the police, sir, and shall do again. Indeed, that is all I can now remember. I remember *only* what Auntie Flo told Tessa and me had happened. There on the spot she told us, and it became so – or rather, it *was* so, it is so, and it always will be. It is the same with Tessa. After all, sir, it is the only version of events that makes any kind of sense.'

'That's my good boy,' said Raisley again. 'Have you any questions for me before we dismiss this wretched business *in aeternum* – for ever and ever, Amen.'

'One question, sir. You will remember that it was required of us that Sarum's death should fulfil two conditions: it should be kindly, and it should make no noise. Well, that hasn't been quite the case, I fear. So is Canteloupe displeased or discontented?'

'No, he is not. Let us, for the very last time, go behind old Flo's version, which is now the truth, to what, for the very last and only time, you might (if you really tried) remember. Sarum, you might conceivably recall at an infinite distance, was enjoying acute pleasure, then suddenly became unconscious and was drowned while still unconscious. What better, what kinder way to go? Would you not agree?'

'Indeed I should.'

'So much for the manner of Sarum's death, which was happy and manful, and therefore pleasing to Canteloupe. But all that is now for ever forgotten, as we come again to the official and public truth, Flo's version as set out to you and Tessa in the grove and on the spot – the version which you and Tessa and Flo, which all of us, now totally believe. You fear lest it will make a noise in the world?'

'Surely, sir.'

'Not much and not for long; and it has the advantage that Sarum's death is now fully and openly explained. He was allowed to drown by a randy and neglectful nurse while she was busy seducing a pretty little ephebe – you. Her own death – the nurse's – followed as a result of the frenzy and confusion caused by Sarum's. Right, Marius?'

'Right, sir,' said Marius, pausing gracefully to accept the congratulations of Colonel 'Buns' Wheelwright, who was famous for having once described Lord Harris as being 'as mean and nasty as a dried up cunt', this to his lordship's face, in the field, and within the hearing of several both senior and junior professionals.

'Right, sir,' said Marius as he and Raisley proceeded.

'Let us concede that most of what happened was matter for scandal,' said Raisley. 'But it was only scandal of the kind that occurs daily and at all levels . . . is so commonplace, indeed, that it has ceased to be scandalous and become merely boring. Tomorrow morning the world will read that the infant son and heir of a marquess was drowned while his nanny had dalliance with a schoolboy

– and that the nanny was suddenly killed by a misadventure which arose from her own shame and panic on being discovered. Because the thing is at a high social level, it will be just that much more spicy an item than the usual run – but not much more, because Canteloupe himself is not remotely implicated, nor is the Marchioness. The only people concerned in the death are a silly slut and a green stripling. And in any case at all the very next day something else will happen to drive this from the public attention – a Cabinet Minister will be found displaying himself in a Waterloo jakes or a miner in Yorkshire will debauch and then strangle all five of his daughters, aged from sixteen down to seven. In a world of scandal, Marius, nothing is scandalous, nothing memorable.

'And, as I say, Sarum's death is now absolutely and openly explained. Had he been sent to some dubious nursing home and there allowed to die of pneumonia, heads would have wagged and tongues clicked and clacked for many years, there would have been talk of callousness and connivance and the convenient disposal, purchased by wealth and privilege, of a degenerate nuisance. As it is, Marius . . . there is just another mishap on a public record which is crammed with them: another child drowned, by no fault of its parents. And so now, I say,' said Raisley Conyngham, raising his hand towards the Campanile as if saluting it, 'the thing is over. There is only the inquest left, and that will not trouble you or the others – safe as you all are in your knowledge of exactly what happened and of your own personal innocence. For how could you, a hot and spunky brat, resist Daisy's seduction? How could poor old Flo help stumbling when she went to rescue the child? And how could Teresa, a humane person if ever there was, not have resisted and

220

thrown off Daisy when she was violently impeding Teresa's efforts to save Sarum? The only true criminal in the story, the nurse, is happily dead – thus removing the only possible complication. And so,' said Raisley Conyngham, lowering his arm slowly as Old Mortality, since it was now the hour of the Retreat, began to toll the passing of Sarum from the Campanile and all the players stood at attention and bowed their heads, 'let Sarum of Old Sarum and his death now be consigned for ever to oblivion. *In Saeculum Saeculorum, O Domine, et tu, O Diabole.* SELAH.'

Carmilla, Len, Milo and the Provost arrived in a hired Daimler just as the players were walking off the field at the close of play. Theodosia now appeared, for the first time since noon, to greet them; and then took away Carmilla and the Provost to explain what had happened to Sarum. At first the Provost cried rather a lot, exclaiming that just as the vengeful tree nymphs had taken his daughter, Baby, so they had taken her child.

'No, Provost,' said Carmilla, who saw her way here. 'These that wanted Sarum were the Nymphs of the Pool, the same that took Hylas to be with them beneath the waters for his beauty's sake. Your grandson has the greatest prize a mortal can win: he has been chosen for the love of the immortal gods.'

This drew a flux of pedantry from Sir Thomas, who pointed out that nymphs, whether of wood or water, were not immortal (they lived for 999 years) and were not gods but at the best demi-. Nevertheless, he took the point

221

much as it was intended, and asked Theodosia to send for Canteloupe.

'Your son has been honoured by the Spirits of the Waters,' said Provost Llewyllyn to Canteloupe when he arrived. 'We too must honour him. As he was christened in the Chapel of Lancaster College, so must he be buried there. There is an Oratory in which those so inclined can pray for the soul of our Founder, the Blessed Henry, who greatly loved children. There we shall make a tomb for Sarum; it shall bear a statue of the boy, naked and seen as Hylas; and on the pedestal we shall have graven: "*Dummodo canities abest morosa*" – he did not live to see the grey years, the years of feeble bone, sour flesh and wilting manhood.'

'Very true, my dear Tom,' said Canteloupe; 'he didn't. Such a memorial to Tullius will be very apt. I take this compliment most kindly, Provost. Please do not forget to consult the Herald's College in order that the arms and bearings may be correct. Sarum's personal motto, as eldest son and heir apparent was *Aucto Splendore Resurgam*: "I shall rise again with increased splendour" – a reference to the fact that (had he lived) he would one day have ceased to be a Baron in order to inherit a Marquisate. In this case, of course, he will inherit only the worm. But I have reason to suppose that it will be entirely apposite that the motto should appear upon his monument.'

Corfu: Castellonet de la Conquista: Walmer

All Fools' Day, 1987

Cocytus
maidan
dominie
furbelows
Narthex
apostasy
fissiparous
oestrus
orison
lashed
stunner
quod
androgynous